LONG TIME NOW

LONG TIME NOW

stories of the dreamtime,
the here and now

Alf Taylor

Magabala Books

First published in 2001 by Magabala Books Aboriginal Corporation,
2/15 Saville Street, P O Box 668, Broome, Western Australia, 6725
Email: info@magabala.com

Magabala Books receives financial assistance from the Commonwealth Government through the Australia Council, its arts funding and advisory body, and the Aboriginal and Torres Strait Islander Commission. The State of Western Australia has made an investment in this project through ArtsWA in association with the Lotteries Commission.

Editor: Dr Rosemary van den Berg
Designer: Narelle Jones
Typeset in: Century Schoolbook 11/13.5
Printed by Hyde Park Press
Cover art: National Land Council Poster © Lin Onus,1988/Licensed by VISCOPY

National Library of Australia
Cataloguing-in-Publication data:

Taylor, Alf. 1947-
Long Time Now: stories of the dreamtime, the here and now.

ISBN 1 875641 68 8

1.Taylor, Alf. 2. Aborigines, South-West of Western Australian - Goldfields, Western Australia, traditional and contemporary social life and customs. 3. Dreamtime, spirituality and images. 4. Nyoongar people, social conditions - urban and rural life. 5. Nyoongar interpersonal relations. 6. Nyoongar idiom. 7. Wongi, urban life. 1. Taylor, Alf. 11. Title.

To my brother Ben Taylor
who has risen above all that I have
written. Good on you – you old
Guildford fox.

Contents

One

Toby and Damper

Toby was staying with his Aunt Flo, a very dear old lady who looked after him as if he were her own son. She was Toby's mother's sister and, naturally, she would care for him after his mum and dad were killed in the horrific road accident when Toby was ten. Aunt Flo was in her middle forties, childless and a very strong Christian lady, who the Nyoongar community respected to the hilt. Toby had been living in Perth with his mother and father prior to the accident and he believed that he should've died along with his parents.

It had been a fine sunny day when the three left Perth for the two and a half hour drive. Aunt Flo had been pleased to see them. Toby and his Nyoongar friends had gone playing in the bush which was where Toby was at his high-spirited best. The bush didn't belong to him, he belonged to the bush. He'd played all afternoon in his beloved bush until it was time for his father to call him. Toby made his way back to Aunt Flo's place.

His mother and father had been waiting in the car for him, ready to make the journey back home. As Toby approached the car, there was something gnawing at him. He hadn't known what it was that was tearing away at him, but seeing Aunt Flo standing by his mother's door and talking to her, Toby had gone directly to his father and mentioned that he wanted to stay with Aunt Flo for the weekend. He'd known that Monday was a public holiday and that his parents would return on Sunday to bring some furniture back to Aunt Flo's. He thought it would be better for him to stay with her until they came back. He'd felt Aunt Flo would be on-side with him, and she'd agreed, leaving his mother and father no alternative but to agree also. This had put great big smiles on his and Aunt Flo's faces and he'd waved good bye to his parents for the last time. It's something he'd never forget. About an hour into the journey, they had had a head-on collision with a semi-trailer on a bend in the road, killing both his mum and dad instantly.

The loss of his parents was traumatic for Toby who found solace in the bush. After school he would dash home, grab a piece of hot damper (if Aunt Flo had just made one) and treacle and into the bush he'd go as fast as his skinny little legs would take him. Once there, he'd find his favourite rock, sit down and hungrily eat his lovely hot damper, letting the crumbs fall to the ground. In fascination, he'd watch the ants clambering over each other to get to the crumbs and carry off bits that looked several times larger than their bodies. Toby often listened to the sounds of the birds which were soothing to his mind and heart. He could tell a bird by its call. They all flocked around him feeding on the crumbs of his damper and, sometimes, a lizard or a spider or a possum would join in. He would laugh at the sight of such a spectacle. Birds, lizards, ants, spiders, a possum and, at one time, even a snake, all chomping on the crumbs of Toby's damper, not attacking each other, just looking at Toby with their eyes full of gratitude.

But this particular day, when Toby had dashed off in his beloved bush with his damper and treacle to sit on his rock, happily eating away, there was a movement which caught his eye. Walking towards an overgrown bush and peering into it, his eyes focused on a little bird with a broken wing. Tenderly reaching into the bush, Toby put his hands gently around the bird, trying, very carefully, to pull it free and trying hard not to disturb its broken wing. Gently pulling the little bird out, he held it to his chest and looked into its eyes. Toby could see only sadness and pain within. Once this small bird had belonged to the freedom of the sky, but now it was handicapped and hiding in the bush. Toby felt for the little bird and, in his heart, he knew he wanted to help it to get back to where it belonged. Holding it close to his heart, he felt the tears well up in his eyes. He felt as though this little bird was his mother, come back to show him how to love and care, to help heal the scars of his hurt. Quickly and carefully he put the little bird back in the bush. He dashed off to find a box, some wire, a bowl and broke some crumbs of damper. He used sunshine powdered milk mixed with water, which he tipped into the bowl for his little friend. After quietly doing these chores, he put the bird in the box and secured the top with wire so no animal, such as a fox, feral cat or whatever, could get at his little friend, snug in its box. Toby then pushed the box back under the bush.

For the next few days, he was very apprehensive about his little friend that he cared for in his spare time. Every morning before and after school, Toby would check on the little creature, always taking a bit of damper and some milk for the bird without Aunt Flo knowing. He didn't tell Aunt Flo, or his friends, about his new little friend. That was his secret. Nobody else knew.

When Aunt Flo gave him damper and honey for his school lunch, Toby would not touch his share, but would save it for his little friend after school. This went on for a couple of weeks. Each time he went to feed the bird, he'd always pull it out of its cage and hold it in the air, so his small friend could flap its wings about. Toby knew its wings were getting stronger and the day must come for him to farewell his little friend from the sky. He knew that day was almost upon him.

One day, the sky was at its bluest and the branches of the trees reached high towards the clouds. The other birds were all perched upon the highest branches, whistling a soft serenade above. As Toby walked through the bush, towards his little friend, he noticed all the leaves were still. No lizards or ants scurried about their daily chores. No breeze tousled his hair. He stopped at the bush that hid the box, pulled it out and gently lifted up his little friend. He nuzzled his nose and lips to its beak and feathers, whispering gently, "I am going to call you Damper. All the damper I have given you will make your little wings strong." The small bird seemed to understand as Toby lifted him into the air. Little Damper fluttered for a while before gathering momentum. Each push of its wings lifted it higher and higher. Toby looked up with tears in his eyes as little Damper flew above the tree tops. It flew out into the open skies before returning to a branch quite close to Toby, who reached out and stroked its soft feathers as if to say good bye. Little Damper flew up to the sky again and to Toby's amazement, he saw all the other birds fly out after him.

The breeze started to rustle the leaves as tears of happiness, tinged with sadness, flowed from Toby's eyes. He tilted his head back to look into the blue yonder and all he could see was a speck on the horizon. Wiping the tears from his eyes, he felt happy. One day, little Damper would lay her own eggs and hatch her own little chicks. He ran through the bush laughing. As he ran, he thought,

I won't have to share my damper anymore. I'll be able to eat the damper Aunt Flo gives me all to myself, and he ran towards home.

Two

The Dream

Toby was a dreamer and, some nights, his dreams would take him far and wide; sometimes out of this world, sometimes into the future and sometimes way back into the past. In his dreams, he would travel the length and breadth of Western Australia; to the lush green grass of the coastal plains, to the rugged hot dry inland areas of the Western Desert, to the spectacular gorges of the Kimberley; and down to the majestic rise of the karri trees in the beautiful south-west of Perth.

Each time on his travels, Brenda was always by his side and they were both dressed in their traditional Aboriginal costumes. Toby, with a tjulep that barely covered his genitals and Brenda, her fresh young breasts exposed to the cool breeze, the sun, rain, his eyes and hands, wore a tjulep, too. With his spear in one hand and Brenda's hand in the other, they would frolic in this virgin land where billabongs, lakes and rivers were at their disposal. Fresh fruit that the land had given birth to, was in a abundance, fresh fish, marrons, crabs and the tender lilies that grew on the river banks. The two young lovers wandered through the peace, tranquility and serenity, going from tribe to tribe, occasionally spearing a kangaroo to take to the tribal festivities. There would be dampers made, kangaroos cooked in the ashes, wild turkeys, fish, marrons and crabs. Indeed the festivities would go on well into the darkest hour of the night, or the lightest hour of the day.

Time was nothing. It didn't dampen their enthusiasm, as they performed the corroboree to the happy sounds of the clap sticks and the clapping of hands, as each foot stamped into the soil. This made the dust rise and linger above the many flames of the fires that surrounded the dancers. Toby would, on occasions, disappear into the darkness of the night and steal a few tender moments with Brenda. Away from prying eyes, he would lavish her young body with tender kisses, whilst the dancers and the flickering flames mingled together as one.

After these few stolen moments with Brenda, he would reappear undetected by the other members of the tribe and steathily take up his position again as he joined the corroboree.

As if by command, the clap sticks and the dancing ceased in the stillness of the night, leaving the crackling of the dancing flames, which erupted from the dry logs on the fire. One of the tribal leaders, a very strong and noble gentleman, stood by the fire and spoke in his Nyoongar tongue for all to hear.

"Greetings my relations, my friends and my in-laws. Tonight we are of one tribe. Although many are scattered all around the bush, mountains, rivers, the plains, to the tallest trees and the rocks to the seas, we are gathered here as one Mob. There is going to be a ceremony in the darkness before the light of the fire. These two young people don't know this is about to happen. But I have spoken to their grandfathers and their grandmothers who, in turn, have spoken to their children. As yet the young people do not know who is involved and have not spoken to their children. But first let me call on the Wise One, the Prophet, the Owl, the Muhbarn Man, the One who can see in the darkness. The One who can see and who can tell you what is about to happen and well before the sun rise. After the Prophet has spoken, I will then call on the young couple and their families to come forward. Then the young couple will go off into the darkness and help to populate our Mob."

I wonder who the lucky young warrior can be, thought Toby, as he glanced around at the other young warriors. They were probably thinking the same as he.

Then the leader started talking again. "But first I want you all to bow your heads. You will not see the Prophet but you will hear his voice, loud and clear and, above all, I want you Mob to take in every word that has been spoken. For he has seen and he knows." The leader sat down with his head bowed, calling the Prophet to speak in the darkness away from the fire-light.

The elders hummed a mournful tune, working towards a crescendo, before stopping abruptly. Then the Mob heard the clear, booming voice of the Prophet, or Mubbarn Man, speak in their Nyoongar tongue. Toby and the other young warriors tried to take a sly peek towards where the elder had indicated that the voice was supposed to have come from. But nothing. Only darkness. The young warriors bowed their heads in anticipation, as the words floated around the Mob, before disappearing into their ears. Toby was shocked by the clear precision of the words as the Prophet spoke.

"You are all living in peace and prosperity. The boundaries of your land you have guarded well; an excellent job. Keep living in peace and harmony, not only within your own tribe, but your neighbouring tribes and their neighbours. But most importantly, take care of your land. Care for it, as you would your mother, father, your children, your elderly and your sick. Kill only the food you want, which is adequate for the tribe. Do not kill for the sake of killing. Burn the dry areas so new vegetation can grow to attract the food. The new tender plants will need sustenance."

There was a pause as if the Prophet was struggling for words before controlling himself and saying in a more audible voice. "The lightning, thunder, rain and the wind has told me that the peace and harmony we are living in now is about to be disrupted. We, of all people, who have been born to this earth and seen our elders laid to rest in this soil and the children who were conceived in this very same soil, will not be able to say genuinely, that this earth is his or her's. I am afraid that this lush green carpet will be snatched from under your feet. Be prepared for the unknown. Don't let your life style accommodate you. It is you who have to accommodate this life. For the rains are getting heavier, they are the tears of the old people, tears that cry for you, tears that you have buried in your soil. But there are people who are about to intrude, invade or just take from you what is rightfully yours. I do not know when this intrusion is about to take place. It could be soon or it could be later; so please be aware of another race of people. Do not trust them, for they will take and destroy."

There was a lot of murmuring amongst the tribe as the Prophet went silent. The elders were bewildered for he had talked in riddles. There are no other race of people living here, only we Aboriginal people. No-one will come to our shores and take what is rightfully ours. There are no such people who would take and not ask, murmured the elders. Then the murmuring was broken by the Prophet. Again the voice coming from the darkness. "You may think that I am confusing you but I, too, feel confused passing this message on to you. I know it sounds like a riddle. But lately the message from the wind is getting stronger and stronger. Even the lightning and thunder are becoming angry with each new day of intrusion. But, like I said, I do not know when this intrusion is about to take place. All I can say is, be very careful. With this, I bid you farewell and now continue your festivities by bringing the young warriors together with their female companions and help to populate your tribe with great numbers. Again I bid you farewell." Once more the wailing sound started, then stopped abruptly after a few minutes. By now, Toby was looking towards the elders, as the high one of ceremonies, was motioned to step foreward. The elder whispered into his ear and sat next to a fire. The high one of ceremonies was dressed in his usual costume of pretty bird feathers and some long reeds and water lilies. He indeed looked a splendour as he raised both arms up to the stars.

When he lowered his arms to his side, he motioned Brenda's grandmother and grandfather to come foreward, which puzzled Toby. Then Brenda's mother and father came forward which caused his heart to miss a couple of beats. I wonder what's going on, he thought, in utter confusion. Brenda was called out by her grandfather in her Nyoongar name. This was becoming more of a mystery. As he watched, her lithe body strode purposely towards her grandmother and stood next to her. He saw the flickering firelight dance on her tender young breasts, over her stomach and travel to her thighs and beyond, for she was illuminated by the firelight.

Toby had seen her exquisite beauty before. She was his, but seeing her loveliness on this night, made him gasp for the cool night air. Toby was dazzled, intoxicated by her sheer beauty. Her aura of loveliness affected everybody that night.

The realisation that Brenda was about to be given to a young warrior made him seethe. "I am going to spear the warrior right between the eyes, whoever he is." he whispered hoarsely to himself. "She is mine and only she could bear me the babies that will give strength to the tribe. She shall give birth to my babies in this soil which is rightfully ours," he whispered again, his eyes still glued to the voluptuous beauty standing in the firelight. He was appalled that she could be given to any one of these young warriors, never to be seen again. "May the spirits help me to secure the woman I desire" he whispered.

To Toby's amazement, his grandmother and grand father were called forward. "This can't be real," he whispered, as his emotions were about to overpower him. Managing to steady himself, he realised this was the joining of he and Brenda to the soil, as his mother and father were called forward. Then shock waves started to tremor throughout his body. Brenda was to be his; his very own. Yet there was something strange going on. The beautiful people standing in front him were beginning to fade, the flames no longer danced in the bright fires and the stars were melting into nothingness. And Brenda? Where was Brenda? As Toby looked around him in bewilderment, he saw her – she was running away from him into the eerie blackness – into the darkness of the night.

Three

Before the Sun

"Wow, Aunty Flo, you sure know how to cook up the biggest feed of kangaroo meat and the loveliest hot damper out!" said Toby with a smug smile on his face. Aunty Flo smiled at young Toby and wondered how she was going to tell him that this year she was sending him to a Catholic school in Perth.

"Yeah," she responded, feeling happy for him, but also feeling rather desolate, not only for herself but, above all, for Toby. She quickly made for the sink and prepared to do the dishes.

Toby sensed that there was something bothering her, but he wasn't too sure on how to approach her. "Aunty Flo?" he questioned her ruefully. "I know there's something bothering you and I'd like to know what it is?" he asked. Getting up from the table and going around to her, he placed an arm around her shoulders and said, "Look, Aunty Flo, you can tell me what's the matter. I will be fifteen this year and you are like a mother to me and I can tell you are worried."

Turning to face Toby, she feigned a smile and said, "We sit at da table an' talk."

Now Toby became very apprehensive and thought, I'm not in trouble with the munartj and none of these Nyoongars around here wanna fight me. Oh . . . no! Don't say Brenda is boojarri! No! no! I'll be a daddy at fifteen. With more urgency in his voice, he said, "Come on and let's sit down."

Sitting across from him and holding his hand, Aunty Flo said, "Toby, you be youn' man now an' you be wise like ol' owl." Smiling.

"You tryin' to tell me Brenda is boojarri," he shouted.

"Course she's not. Who bin tellin' you?" she asked.

"Thank fuck'" said a relieved Toby.

"Don't you dare swear in dis house. Dis is da Lord's house. You know I don't like um swearin' in dis house."

Toby was quite annoyed with himself because he never swore in front of Aunty Flo, whose faith to the Lord she had tried to instil in Toby, but to no avail. He respected her wishes and even went to church with her, but going to church didn't rub off on him. He used swear words in the right context and only around his mates. "Look, Aunty Flo, you know I'm sorry. It just slipped out."

"I gib you 'slipped out'. I can still belt you, you know dat," she said quite angry with Toby. "Anyway, what I wanna tell you," she said, regaining her composure, "is dat you gonna go to school in Perth dis year."

"What!" he said, in a surprised voice.

Before he could fire questions at her, she went on to tell him while he was still in a dazed state. "I bin talk to welfare an' I sign da papers so you can go to a Catholic school down dere an' lib in a Nyoongars' hostel for boys. I want you to be a good reada an' writa. 'Course I know you can talk good, but dis readin' and writin', no good. Now you bin hear me proper good an' no swearin'," she told him and felt good within herself for getting it out in the open. She prepared herself for the barrage of questions that was about to be fired at her.

Toby was in a state of shock. He was totally bewildered.

She looked at Toby and saw his mouth moving, but no words came, only sounds of hysteria. "You be orright," she asked with concern.

Pulling his hands away from his face, he looked at her rather quizzically and said, "Did I hear you say Catholic school, Perth and Nyoongars' hostel all in the same breath?"

"Dus true, my boy," she responded.

"I don't understand, I mean, you being a very strong born-again Christian lady and you sending me to a Catholic school in Perth; I thought that all the different religious groups had all different gods." he said, looking at her rather vaguely.

"Now, dus all nonsense. We all pray to da same gawd to get to heben," she laughed.

With confidence, she went on to tell him that she had arranged for him to go to school in Perth, through Community Welfare here, and stay at a hostel for young Nyoongars – boys, of course. The high school wasn't far from where he was going to stay.

It all fell into place for Toby. The big puzzle started to form pictures in his head. The more she talked, the more he started to put it all together. What she had done, did annoy Toby. She could've talked to him about it because this was his life she was arranging, not a vase of flowers, he thought. But, then again, she always made decisions for Toby, without consultation. Toby just shrugged it off.

She said, "Da Lord tell me for you to go to school in Perth. An' your readin' and writin' be proper good."

Toby agreed with her. It was now a matter of telling Brenda. I'm sure she'll understand, he thought. But then again, she was only fourteen and in grade seven. Here I am nearly fifteen and in Year Eight and going to a school in Perth this year. His first thoughts were yorgahs, parties and more yorgahs. Fuck the drugs and gerbah, just give me tuppies, tuppies and more tuppies.

"You bin listen' to what I bin sayin'" she scolded him.

"Uh . . . yeah, course" said Toby, snapping back to reality. Thank God Aunty Flo can't read my thoughts otherwise I'd be burning in the flames of hell, he thought.

"You look like you not bin listenin'," she snapped at Toby. "I bin talkin' to myself, unna?" she asked.

"No, no, my dear old Mother/Aunty. It's just that I'll have to come to terms with it," he said smiling.

"You be not sad, den?" she questioned. "You know, like leabin' Brenda an' all your 'lations?" she enquired.

"No, of course not. Maybe I'll miss Brenda and, of course, you, my number one lady. And, of course, Uncle Jacko, the number one buntji man." He laughed, making Aunty Flo go into fits of laughter. Between laughs Toby managed to splutter, "I wonder where that old buntji man is?"

Managing to subdue her laughter, she told him, "Dey bin tell me him bin gone to Meekatharra. Him bin chasin' all da yorgahs up dere."

"I think it's the other way around. It's all the yorgahs chasin' him around," Toby said, also managing to control his laughter. He could just imagine Uncle Jacko up in Meekatharra. He would be the life and soul of any party. He's the only man who could turn sorrow into laughter and depression into joy, or turn a scowl into a smile. Muntjin some Yamatji yorgah up that way. Old Brickwall Oswald Jackson loved his women . . . colour or creed didn't bother him, as long as he end up inside their pants, thought Toby, smiling.

"What for you bin smilin'?" she asked, "You might be too happy to go."

"I am happy to go," he said "but I am not happy to go because I'll be leaving everyone I love behind."

"Yeah, dus true, but you go down an' show dees Nyoongars dat you gonna be a good reada and writa, unna."

"Course," he said eagerly.

"Dus good den," she replied. "Go an' tell your mob you be goin' Perth soon. Might be next week."

Toby got up from the table, kissed Aunty Flo and said to her, "I'll go and tell my mob and I hope Brenda can see some sense in it all."

Stepping into the warm night and wondering how Brenda was going to take this, he heard dogs barking around different Nyoongars' houses. I wish Uncle Jacko was here. He'd be able to talk to me on the subject of yorgahs. I couldn't talk to Aunty Flo, like I can talk to Uncle Jacko, he thought. He went into various Nyoongars' houses and told them of his future plans and how he regretted leaving his mob.

But surprisingly enough, many of the Nyoongars knew of his going away long before he did. Being in a small country town, yarns spread pretty quickly and this had become rather upsetting for him. He was confused and bewildered. He wondered if Brenda knew and, if she did, what did she think of it. As he made his way to her place, in the warm night, he saw her sitting under the light on the front steps of the verandah. His thoughts were in disarray as he approached her. I've got to get my brains together, he thought, and say the right things to her. Obviously, she's heard that I'll be going to school in Perth.

"What's the matter, Brenda?" he asked.

She peered into the darkness and turned away from him as he sat down beside her.

"You tell me," she said, not looking at him.

"Brenda, look, I've just found out about all this a couple of minutes ago from Aunty Flo," he said.

"Yeah, I bet," she said in a sombre manner.

"True as my Mum and Dad," he pleaded.

This brought a response from her as she turned to look at him. She believed that he was telling the truth, because he never spoke of his mum and dad unless he was telling the truth. So when he mentioned his parents, she knew he was telling the truth. On one occasion, a cousin of her's said she went out with Toby and had spent the night with him. He was drunk at the time. She had confronted him about this a few days later and he had sworn black and blue that he hadn't. He had used the same words then — 'True as my Mum and Dad.' She had followed up the yarn which was disturbing her and, finally, she had found out that this girl was full of bullshit. As one of her other cousins told her. 'No, don't believe her. She's a little trouble-maker and the biggest slut out.' Toby had gone on a weekend excursion and never came into contact with her. When this fact became known to Brenda, she apologised profusely to him.

"Look, Brenda, you should know this little town fulla Nyoongars. Every one else knew that I was going to Perth except me," he said.

Moving closer and putting her arm around him, she said softly, "I'm sorry, Toby. I thought you knew and was too excited to tell me."

"No, no, you'd be the first one to know. It's just Aunty Flo has made all these plans for me and not even tellin' me about them. And to make matters worse, she tells all these other Nyoongars."

This got them both laughing and hugging each other and she whispered softly in his ear, "Oh, Toby, I love you so much and it hurt real bad when these other Nyoongars told me that you were going away."

Pulling her face to his and brushing away a tear from her eyes, he said, "It is I who love you so much and my heart belongs to you and only you."

With these words spinning inside her heart, she kissed his lips fervidly, searching to kiss out those beautiful words she longed to come from his mouth. She felt his lips searching her's and his left hand gently massaging the nape of her neck, as his right hand gently caressed her face. She thought that she was going to explode, as she squirmed under his hot wanton lips that muffled any sound that was coming from the bottom of her heart. She prayed this kiss would last forever. She felt his intensity was about to erupt as the hot molten lava of love spread through to her. She was practically exploding herself with the excitement, passion and happiness which had engulfed her.

"Please . . . Toby . . . no, please," her voice began to quiver as she tried to untangle herself from his grasp. "No, please, Toby, we've got to stop," she pleaded, trying to take control of herself and the situation.

"Brenda, oh, Brenda, I want you so bad it hurts," he begged.

Her want for him was overwhelming. She gasped and took in great big lungfuls of air.

"Toby, time to go home," a voice suddenly cut into the stillness of the night.

Aunty Flo, they both thought, peering into the darkness. She stepped into the light and said to Brenda, "I take Toby home. You okay, girl?"

Nodding her head and getting up quickly, Brenda dashed inside, leaving Toby in a very embarrassing position. Getting up rather quickly and turning his back on Aunty Flo, he adjusted his clothes in the appropriate order and said, "Go along, Aunty Flo, I'll be there in a minute."

He heard her shuffle away on the gravel pavement and wanted to scream his love for Brenda at her door. Then realizing every Nyoongar's dog along the street would cause a commotion, he thought it wouldn't be appropriate at this particular hour. He wandered off in the direction of Aunty Flo's house and, feeling rather defeated, went into his room. He lay down just in a pair of jocks and wondered what might have been if only Aunty Flo hadn't intervened . . .

Suddenly, a voice called out from somewhere, "Toby, you get and go to school!" The voice was familiar. Was it his mother's voice, he wondered, afraid of the unknown.

"Toby, you hear me or what? 'Cause um is gunna come and give it to you and you know what for, if you don't get up."

Opening his eyes slowly, he blinked rapidly a couple of times to adjust to his whereabouts. Looking up at the ceiling then at the curtain on the window, which seemed to be laughing at him, he realised that he was back where he belonged at Aunty Flo's, who was practically screaming the door down.

"'urry up an' git up dis minute," she roared.

"Yeah, I'm comin'," he called back, as the commotion quietened down outside his door. Getting up quickly, he headed for the bathroom to get ready . . . for what? he thought.

Walking into the kitchen, he grabbed a cup of tea and sat down at the table with Aunty Flo, who asked him, "You orright or what, 'cause you bin sick and went to bed early, 'bout sundown."

It was Toby who gave her a quizzical look and asked, "You not sending me to a Nyoongar hostel and a Catholic school? I thought I was going to have beautiful young nuns teachin' me what they shouldn't be teachin' me, and the pious monks tellin' me that lookin' at pretty Nyoongar girls lustfully would get me seven days in hell," with a sneer in his voice.

"What!" Aunty Flo exploded, "What you talk 'bout Catholic school an' what hostel you talk 'bout?" she enquired with hostility.

"Then, you're not sending me to Perth," he asked again, to make himself quite clear and wanting her to say the words he wanted to hear.

"You won't be going anywhere," she laughed. "I promised your mother's spirit that I will look after and care for you as long as it takes me," she said in a solemn voice. "But you know what, I bin thinkin', you musta had a dream las' night, 'cause you bin sick early and I bin tell you to go to sleep. I bin worried for you. Tell me your dream."

With a laugh, he told her, "I can't, Aunty Flo, but I can tell you, Brenda and I were saying a lingering goodbye and things were getting hot. You woke me up too soon, before the sun."

Four

Toby

"Hey, Toby, how about coming out and giving us a hand with some hay carting tomorrow?" said Big Merv, hoping he'd say yes because he was short of a couple of men. Big Merv knew if he got Toby to come out, he would be getting a good honest worker.

"You for real?" said Toby, "I get my dole cheque tomorrow and at the moment I've got the shakes real bad," for he knew if Merv wanted him, he'd take the hint.

"Been on the plonk?"

"Naw, just beer. When I'm getting over it, it tends to knock me around a bit."

"Christ, Toby, for a young man, you sound like a real booze artist. How old are you now? Twenty-six? Twenty-seven?"

"Twenty-four next month," said Toby, feeling like he was fifty-four.

"Okay, I can lend you ten bucks, but I'll take it out of your wages tomorrow. Anyway it's four or five hours work left out there. You'll be back in time to cash your dole cheque at the bank."

"My dole goes straight to the bank."

"Right then," said Big Merv, handing over the ten dollars. "I'll be around early so take it easy on the piss, they say it's going to be hotter than today. So keep your energy for tomorrow," said Merv as he headed out of the shade of the verandah to his vehicle.

"Yeah, see ya tomorrow," shouted Toby, as Merv pulled away.

Jesus, thought Toby, it's hot enough now and it's only ten thirty. We're gonna be boiling by this afternoon. Tomorrow is gonna be worse. Why wasn't I born a fish, duck, platypus or even a frog?

"What Big Merv want?" said Aunty Flo, as she walked on to the verandah with Toby.

"Wants me to go out tomorrow, finish some hay carting off," replied Toby.

"You'll be getting your cheque tomorrow, what for you go out?"

"So I won't be down the pub drinking," said Toby, getting annoyed and then realizing he shouldn't have snapped at this old lady, who had looked after him since his mother and father got killed in a road accident.

He was ten when she took him in. She was Mum's eldest sister, so naturally she took over his life the best she could. Aunty Flo was a widow and childless and she always said the Lord meant it that way.

"I'm off, Aunty," said Toby.

"Where you going, down to the pub?" said Aunty Flo. "All Nyoongar kids today, soon as they get out of their nappies, straight to the pub. Ask them to come to church they say, 'No, I can't, gotta sore ankle'." She was shaking her head as she walked back into the house, leaving Toby deep in thought. It's been fourteen years today since Mum and Dad died in that accident. I don't know. Something wrong, but what?

Heading for the pub, he could almost taste the cold amber fluid as he fingered the ten dollar note in his pocket. Didn't take him long to find his way into the cool beautiful air inside. Stepping in from thirty five degree celsius to a moderate twenty just about took his breath away.

"Middy, thanks," said Toby, as he put the ten dollars on the bar.

"Hey, Toby, get your cheque today?" shouted Willie standing at the pool table.

"Naw, Big Merv lent me ten bucks," he said, his shaking hand grabbing for the middy, raising it quickly up to his lips and gulping the beer down as his eyes wandered the bar. Few Nyoongars today, like to know who got their money, might cadge a few more bucks. One thing about being a Nyoongar, he'll never see another Nyoongar stuck. Thank God, I'm a blackfella. Oh, oh, here comes Brenda.

She was swivelling her hips as she came towards him. "Buy me a beer, Toby, and I'll make your night," said Brenda, standing close.

"Jesus, Brenda, you're a bum," said Toby, stepping back.

"Yeah, you like rubbing your hands over it," said Brenda with a real sexy smile.

"No, not that bum. Aw, forget it. Two middies, thanks," said Toby, as he pushed the money to the barmaid.

"You don't look too good, Toby," said the barmaid, making for the glasses and money.

"Yeah, don't feel too good either, got the shakes real bad."

"Here, this will steady you down," she said, as she put the beer in front of him.

"Thanks," he said, as he passed one to Brenda, "Cheers!"

He felt good as the cold amber fluid went down his throat in big gulps, even his blood started to circulate through his body. God, I think I can understand how a junkie must feel after getting a hit. His body seemed to relax as each drop went down at a quick pace.

"Come on, woman, drink up," he said.

"Hell, Toby, I can't drink that fast," as she put her hand down the front of her dress, quickly pulling out a twenty dollar note.

"Shit, where in the hell that come from, the left or the right?" said Toby, with a slight smile on his face.

"Would you believe I've a third one that holds

all the money?" said Brenda smiling.

"Last time I felt, you had two," said Toby, warming up to the conversation.

"I got my dole cheque this morning. I don't want this mob to know, especially that brother of mine, Willie," said Brenda.

Toby looked across at the other Nyoongars in the bar. They were far more interested in playing pool and darts than in him and Brenda, so he quickly slipped the twenty dollar note to the barmaid for a refill. The barmaid understood these people, so when she brought the change and the beer back, she put the beer on the bar, and just as quick, she slipped the change into Toby's hand all in one movement, even beating Willie's sharp eyes.

Willie couldn't stand it anymore. He put his cue stick down, saying to Morrie, "I'm going over to Toby and Brenda, have your shot if you want."

"I'll wait till you come back," said Morrie as he chalked his cue stick.

"Hey, you two, why don't youse come over and join us mob or we too black for youse?" said Willie, grinning.

"Naw, I'm still a bit crook. A couple of more beers and I'll give youse a game," said Toby, looking at Brenda.

"You get your money today, sis?"

"No, Bro', Toby is shouting," she said, looking at Toby, hoping that he'd agree with her.

"I told you, Merv lent me ten bucks, plus Aunty Flo gave me some."

"What? She lent you money for beer? This world must be coming to an end. She strong Christian, that old girl."

"Come on, Willie," shouted Morrie. "These two want a game of doubles directly," pointing to Mocco and Sam.

"Morrie's got his money today, that's why I'm sticking with him," said Willie, making off.

"I reckon that brother of yours can smell a dollar coin a mile away."

"Yeah, he sure can, where's my change?" said Brenda, slipping her hand under cover.

"Here," she said, "keep ten dollars. You can give it to me tomorrow or cut it out tonight."

"Is that a promise or a threat?" said Toby as he grabbed for his middy.

"Ahh, this is getting better. If I keep this up, no way will I be fronting tomorrow. You're not helping, Brenda, you should be saying have a few beers, go home and be up bright and early to kick off the day."

"Look, Toby, you got your marbles and I've got mine," she said laughing.

"Yeah, that's true, let's say we lose our marbles and do something weird and wonderful tonight, what ya reckon?"

"Hmm, I kinda like that," said Brenda, feeling the warmth spreading though her body.

By this time, Toby was running on high and tapping his feet to a Neil Diamond rock ballad coming from the juke box. This particular song he remembered very well from a pub in Perth. He had his eye on a spunky yorgah, went over and chatted her up, spent about thirty dollars on her and thought he was on a winner. In walked her man with three of her brothers and proceeded to punch the piss out of him. I'll never forget this song, thought Toby. Every time I hear it, I can still feel the pain and that was six months ago.

Willie, Morrie, Mocco and Sam came over to them. "Let's say we grab a carton, have a drink out at the old reserve," said Willie.

"If Toby go, I go," said Brenda in no uncertain terms.

"Yeah, sis, you can come. It'll be cheaper getting a carton and going to the old reserve than sitting here," said Willie, making his point.

"What, in this heat? The bottles'll melt, not counting us," said Toby, feeling uneasiness going through his body. He knew something was telling him to stop, but the grog he'd consumed was giving him a false sense of security. It overpowered his innermost feelings and he said, "Yeah, I guess you're right, but how in the hell we're gonna get out there."

"Sam's gotta car," chipped in Morrie, who was fishing in his pockets to get hold of the notes.

"Let's go, then," said Toby, grabbing Brenda's hand.

"Hey, wait a minute," said Brenda, pulling back from Toby.

"I'm not gonna be the only yorgah there."

"You won't be. Sam will take us out first. Then he'll come back to pick up Julie, Sue and Mary," said Willie.

"There'll be yorgahs there. I've already spoken to Sue, she said they'll go," putting his sister at ease. Not that she needed to be put at ease. She had her sights on Toby, whether she got him or not, only time would tell.

Toby went out with women, but never committed himself to just one, for he was like a bee going from flower to flower, sucking the nectar from them, then flying home to his hive feeling well satisfied.

"Right," said Willie, "all the goods are in. Let's get going." Toby and Brenda jumped in front with Sam.

"Jesus, Sam, you reckon this old heap-o-shit will get us out there?" said Toby wondering why in hell was he talked into it.

"Course it will. This car will take us to Kal and back," said Sam, as he started the motor up, grinning from ear to ear.

"This thing sounds as if it's running on one spark plug," said Toby, wincing at the noise coming from the motor.

"Don't worry, the other spark plugs will catch up to the one working on its own," said Sam, smiling to the blokes at the back.

"Yeah, Toby, you can't beat a Valiant."

"Looks to me," said Toby, "that somebody already beaten it about the body with a crowbar or an axe." Sam was too busy putting the Valiant into motion to take any notice of Toby's smart remarks.

As they chugged off, there was a shout of joy from Sam. He didn't believe he was moving. There was a sickening noise coming from the motor. Yes, if the cops got hold of this car, they would blow it to pieces just to keep Australia beautiful. Reckon the occupants would go with it.

The old reserve was about five kilometres out of town and mainly a down hill run, so it didn't take long before it came into view. As they got there, Sam pulled under a shady tree where there was a slight breeze rustling the leaves in the late afternoon.

Some relief, thought Toby. Not as good as the pub but, at least, we're out of the law's way.

"My, my," said Toby, getting out. "So peaceful and quiet out here," looking around the reserve.

"You know, once our ancestors played, talked, loved and made very wise decisions here! Their children's voices filled this old place with laughter of joy and cries of happiness."

"Jesus, Toby, you're a dreamer alright," said Brenda, wondering what it would have been like living out here with no hot water or septic system and all the tribe living in humpies. She shivered at the thought.

"Forget about the past and live for the present," said Willie, grabbing a bottle and knocking the top off with his teeth. He held it in the air saying, "The white man maketh, the black man drinketh."

"This is all I live for, a cold bottle of beer," said Morrie, grabbing the bottle from Willie.

"You blokes are in the rats," said Brenda, thinking she was living in the past, present and future all at once with these blokes.

"Look," said Sam, "Just give us a bottle and I'll go and pick these yorgahs up."

"Yeah, don't be long, and bring another carton back," said Morrie, pulling out a twenty dollar note.

"What about juice?" said Sam, climbing into the car with his bottle.

"Here's another five dollars then," said Morrie, passing over twenty five dollars. Sam started the old Valiant up, then proceeded to rev the shit out of the old bomb. They all cheered as he took off in a cloud of dust as the old bomb groaned out of sight.

"Willie, where did Sam get that heap-o-shit from? I think I've seen that car somewhere before," said Toby, trying to remember where. Willie burst out laughing.

"Course you seen it, Uncle Jacko had it. Have a guess what Sam swapped for it." Laughing louder.

"What?" said Toby, also begining to laugh.

"His colour TV and a kangaroo dawg," said Willie, amidst the laughter.

"You're joking," said Toby, bending over laughing.

"No, no, true as Jesus. Ask Mocco," said Willie, laughing louder.

"Yeah, true as Gawd," said Mocco, trying to make the sign of the cross on his chest, but it was difficult because Morrie and Brenda were laughing themselves hoarse.

"Does Sam's woman know about it?" said Toby, trying to stop himself from laughing.

"That's the best part of it. You see, she and the baby went down to Roelands last night for a Christian meeting, it goes all day today, she'll be home tomorrow. She don't even know," which got them all laughing again.

"I can't get over it," said Toby, "Imagine swapping the family TV and a mangy mutt for a car not worth twenty dollars. Mutt, yeah, TV, no."

Uncle Jacko wouldn't gain from the swap. He had often seen his niece, who is Sam's woman, going up to the surgery and carrying the baby on her hip. Uncle Jacko would often say to her. "Never mind, niecey, Uncle Jacko will buy a car one pension day and I'll give it to you, so you can take my little granny up in style." Uncle Jacko would give the dog away to any Nyoongar who wanted it, but the TV will go for a carton, a flagon and ten dollars if he was lucky. The TV would do the full cycle of Nyoongar families before it would eventually get back to Sam and his wife.

They sat drinking for a couple of hours talking about the weather, cricket, their ancestors, today's living, tomorrow's conditions, this coming footy season and above all, about Sam's car, which always brought a laugh. They were getting low on beer.

"I wonder where that Sam got to," said Toby, grabbing for the last bottle.

"He should have been back by now," said Brenda, listening for the sickening sound of Sam's car.

"You reckon he broke down?" asked Morrie

"I wouldn't be at all surprised," said Toby.

"Yeah, but he'd have plenty of time to walk into town, get the grog and get someone to bring him back," said Willie, scratching his head.

"This is our last bottle," said Mocco taking a swig.

"We might have to walk back," said Brenda.

"Anyway it's getting cooler now, won't be long before the sun go down," said Mocco.

"I'm going for a leak," said Toby, getting up and heading towards the bush. He got into the trees out of sight of the others and he was standing there, when a big branch broke off, just missing him. Funny, he thought, no wind. Why would a strong branch like that just decide to break off and nearly hit me? Maybe our ancestors' spirits are trying to tell me something or they're angry with us because we are drinking here. As Toby walked back he was very seriously thinking about what happened. Shall I tell them? Naw, thought Toby, they don't believe in this blackfella stuff anymore. Either they are hooked on booze or this religion has got 'em. Naw, I won't tell em.

"I thought you walked into town," said Brenda.

"Hey, what's the matter, Toby? You look like you zipped your old fella up," said Willie, laughing.

"I'm alright," said Toby, sitting down next to

Brenda and putting his arm around her. She leaned on Toby's shoulder and felt his body jumping.

"You sure you okay, Toby? I can feel you shaking all over," said Brenda, with concern in her voice.

"You seen a devil or something?" said Mocco, looking towards the bushes.

"Like Willie said, he must've got his old fella zipped up," said Morrie, bumping Willie.

"I'll tend to it tonight," whispered Brenda, into Toby's ear. Toby grabbed and kissed her, not a wild passionate kiss, but a soft lingering, loving kiss, for he felt hopeless. He felt his spirit was trying to tell him something. What? What? His mind screamed out in his head.

"Any beer left?" said Toby, pulling away from Brenda.

"Mouthful left," said Willie, as he passed the bottle. Toby finished the last remaining drop. He had just put the bottle down when the police van came into view.

"Christ," said Mocco, "We could be sitting out in the middle of the desert drinking, these coppers'd still manage to find us."

"Yeah," said Willie.

The police van pulled up in front of them, the sergeant got out followed by the constable.

"Drunk all the grog?" said Sarge, sitting on his haunches, eyeing the empties.

"Yeah," said Morrie, "Look, Sarge, we bring our drink out here 'cos we don't want to cause trouble in town. We're on our own here, nobody to bother us."

"Yes, I quite agree with it. Make it easier for me. I wish a few of the others would do the same, instead of fighting and swearing around in town."

"What is it, Sarge?" said Toby. He knew the Sarge was trying to tell them something and that he had not come out to the old reserve for nothing.

"It's Sam," said the Sarge.

"You got him for drunk driving," said Brenda, her chest tightening up.

"I only wish I had, Brenda."

Toby knew what was coming up next. It all fell into place, the broken branch, his restless spirit, Sam taking so long. Sam won't be back in body. In spirit, yes.

The Sarge continued, "Sam has had an accident at the old bridge on his way back."

"Anyone else in the car with him?" said Brenda, trembling all over.

"No, he was by himself, with all the grog in the back. His car went out of control and over the bridge."

There was deathly silence, as they all expected what was coming next.

"I'm afraid he's dead. Killed instantly," said the Sarge, glad he was able to get that out into the open. Toby, Brenda, Mocco, Morrie and Willie, all huddled together, arms around each other and looked up to the heavens and cried openly, as the Sarge and the constable moved away from the sad mob, shaking their heads. When he knew they were settling down, he said to Toby, "I can give you people a lift into town if you want," opening the back of the van.

"Thanks, Sarge," said Toby.

"Where do you all want to jump off?" said the constable.

"Aunty Flo's," said Toby.

"Okay," he said as he closed the door behind them.

Five

Brenda

Blood trickled from her nose to her mouth as she cowered against the bedroom wall, praying he wouldn't hit her again. He stood towering over her, fist clenched, snarling down at her. "You fuckin' bitch, go to Toby if you want. But you're not takin' the kids. I reared Tomby up from a little fella. He's mine, not Toby's. And you know Ryan and Gina are mine legally. If you take them, I'll come after you and kill you."

"Please, Mocco," she whimpered, wiping the blood from her mouth. "Toby's been gone for five years now. He's not even a memory anymore." She knew that was a lie. He will always be a part of me, she thought.

"You fuckin' better 'member that," he snarled, staggering back, then quickly throwing out his right hand to find the wall for support. He regained his balance and shouted at her.

"Gimme some money. I wanna go down the pub. Hurry up, you fuckin' bitch."

She peeked at him through a veil of tears, noticed some distance between her and Mocco, and quickly wiped her eyes. Her hand was like a flash as it dived down to her bra. Holding a ten dollar note in her outstretched hand, she got up and planted her two feet firmly on the floor.

"Here," she sobbed, "take it. That's all I have left for the kids." Eyeing the money, he regained his composure. With a smile on his face, he snatched it out of her hand and headed toward the door.

"You'd better be here, bitch, when I get home," he shouted at her, slamming the front door behind him and staggering off into the darkness.

The crickets knew when he was out drinking. They always chirped pretty loudly, but this particular night they chirped even louder, as if to soothe the hurt, anger and hate which had been building up for the last few years.

Funny, she thought, making her way to the bathroom, even the breeze on this warm night is embracing me.

She splashed cold water on her face, wincing as it came in contact with her bloody nose and bruises. Gingerly drying herself with a towel and looking at her face in the mirror, she whispered, "This is it, Brenda, you're leaving him tonight. I am sick and tired of this life. I'll have to leave the kids behind. If I take them, he'll track us down and kill us all."

Tears burst from her eyes when she mentioned the children. As an afterthought, she whispered determinedly, "Please let death claim me tonight." She turned away from the tormented face looking at her.

Peeking into the kids room, she saw everything was quiet and peaceful. Tomby and Ryan shared one bed, Gina occupied another on her own across from the boys. Without making a sound, she went across to the boys. Looking at Tomby she whispered, "Toby, he is your son. After you left for the Goldfields or somewhere, you left a seed inside me that flowered into Tomby. He's going on for six now, Toby, and he looks exactly like you. Those big, beautiful, brown eyes are yours."

"Why did you feel guilt about Sam's death? It was an accident, even Sam's woman told you that and Uncle Jacko said it too. If only you had stayed. I'm sure we'd have a big family by now. I'm living with Mocco. He was one of your mates, but he turned out a real bastard. He knew I was pregnant when I went to live with him. He said he was going to look after Tomby, but after Ryan was born he treated him like shit." She kissed Tomby, then Ryan and Gina. The kids did not stir as her lips came in contact with their soft skin. She whispered furiously, "I love you, kids, please forgive me if I am not here in the morning."

She made her way back to her room on unsteady legs, to fall on the bed and cry. The walls of her reservoir of pain tumbled down and she felt all the agonising tears fall free.

She thought of Toby in the midst of her ache. "Toby, Toby," she called his name softly within the darkness of the room. Her mind went back to those blissful days of love. The stolen glances. A quick kiss before Aunty Flo walked into the room. He making love to her with his eyes when all the relatives were around. She remembered their first love-making very clearly. He had taken her out to the old reserve on a warm summer's evening. The wild flowers were wilting under the hot sun. He'd stopped the ute under the trees and they'd attacked each other's mouths ferociously. No words were spoken. He led her to the wilting wild-flowers that crackled under the weight of her body as she'd undressed in a frenzy. She'd felt the warm soil under her bare skin as he gently lowered his naked body on to hers. The smell of eucalyptus leaves lingered in the air. The crickets, their only audience, put on a concerto for them. The music exploded in their brains.

"Yeah, Toby," she whispered, "he's still jealous of you. If I only can find you again."

She fell into a restless sleep where she could see a horrifying dream performing inside her head. Screaming silently, she saw a distorted face with distorted teeth biting great chunks of flesh out of her stomach. Grinning hideously, it proceeded to lap at her blood and the innermost part of her soul.

Like a bolt of lightning cracking in her mind,

this was replaced with tranquility and ecstasy as her dream took her back forty thousand years. She and Toby were frolicking naked through virgin forest. He was the king of the tribe and she was his queen. They splashed under waterfalls and paddled in billabongs. Everything was at their disposal, then her tranquil dream was shattered by a banging on the door.

Instinctively she made for the wardrobe to grab her clothes, saying softly to herself. "Gotta get away, gotta get away." Her brain was not responding to her actions until she recognised a shrill voice, which she immediately recognised, "Brenda! Open dis door! Munartj here with me."

What Aunty Flo and Munartj doing here? she thought. I hope the bastard's in jail.

"Yeah, comin', Aunty Flo," she called, trying to adjust her thoughts to the here and now.

Opening the door, she could see Aunty Flo was in a state of shock and immediately shouted at her. "What happened? Why Munartj here? Tell me what happened? What's going on?" She felt her stomach was being ripped open again by that distorted face. And she was going into shock.

Aunty Flo composed herself and put her arms around Brenda as she replied, "Something bad happened to dat man of yours, he gone now."

This old Nyoongar woman, Toby's blood Aunty, is confusing me, Brenda thought, as she started to perspire.

"Sit down, girl," the old lady whispered, gently guiding her to a chair. She added, "Munartj wanna tell you something."

Looking into the policeman's face, Brenda saw his mouth moving but no words seemed to be coming out.

"I'm . . . accident . . . beer . . . railway line . . . train . . . sorry."

This is weird, she thought, why Aunty Flo crying next to me? She looked at the policeman's back making its way out the door. Now all these Nyoongars coming in shaking my hand. Why are they all wailing? Kissing and hugging me. Go away, go away! her mind screamed out, leave me alone. What Aunty Flo talking about now, two words sound like Serapax and water. A tablet was put into her mouth, followed by a glass of water pressed to her lips, washing the tablet down her throat into her stomach. Then slowly everyone was disappearing before her eyes. The distorted face was fading. She was floating, the lights inside her head were being turned off. Darkness inside my head, a prisoner of my mind.

The first light of dawn came early. Brenda stretched around and looked for Mocco, wrinkling up her nose. Good, the bastard's in jail. I'm not going to bail him out, let him stop there, she thought. What a horrible dream I had last night.

Aunty Flo walked in with a big mug of hot tea. She looked terrible, her eyes were all red, as if she never had any sleep last night.

"The kids play up?" Brenda asked.

"No. My girl, got something to tell you," she replied.

Looking at her downcast eyes, Brenda knew it was no dream, "What? What?" she screamed and began to sob uncontrollably.

"Tell you after, girl," was the old lady's reply and she quietly left the room.

She heard people knocking on the door and heard Aunty Flo turning them away in a gracious manner. Then, later, she heard Aunty Flo knock on the door and call out, "Can I come in, girl?"

"Come in, Aunty," she called back in a hoarse voice. Aunty Flo came in and held her hand.

"You right now?" she whispered. Brenda shook her head. "Tell me all, Aunty."

"You know when he left here last night?"

How could I forget that, Brenda thought. Aunty Flo went on to say that Mocco was drinking in the pub till closing time. Then he got a carton of beer.

"That's not right," sobbed Brenda. "He only had ten dollars on him."

Apparently, the police had told Aunty, he borrowed twenty dollars off his mate and got a carton of beer. He was staggering across to the other side of town for a drink with some of his mates. He was on his own.

Aunty Flo went on to tell her, "If somebody was there with him, he would have been alive now. As he was crossing the line, he stumbled and fell, hitting his head on the tracks and knocking himself out. About half an hour later, a goods train came along and mangled him up. You know what was the funny thing?" said Aunty Flo, shaking her head.

"What?" replied Brenda in barely a whisper.

"That carton fell out of his hand and landed on the other side of the line and only broke three of the bottles. Uncle Jacko identified the ring on his finger, with his and your name on it. That's all they can tell – oh, I'm sorry, girl," said the old lady. They grabbed each other and cried.

The children were told. Tomby, she could not work out, he was like Toby. Don't think he wants to face up to reality. Ryan's five and Gina's our baby doll, they're much too young to understand. When they get older, I'll tell them.

It was a big funeral on that particular day. Nyoongars came from all over the wheatbelt area, far and near. Some came from Perth and some from down the Southwest. Brenda was hoping Toby wouldn't be there as it would make her very uncomfortable. Mocco's death had been in the funeral notices in the paper. She was glad when Toby didn't turn up.

A couple of weeks after the funeral, Brenda was moping around the house when Aunty Flo took her aside and said, "Come on, now, girl, what you gonna do?"

"I don't know, Aunty," Brenda replied truthfully.

"Now you tell Aunty Flo the truth, girl, how you feel."

"Oh, Aunty," she burst out crying. "I didn't want it to happen this way. I wanted to leave him on that night. Why didn't he leave me?" she sobbed.

"Now, now, girl," responded Aunty Flo, getting up to comfort her. "The Lord taketh and the Lord giveth, the Lord knows what He's doing."

Brenda knew this old lady believed what she was talking about. She'd often told Toby off for not going to church.

Then she was startled as Aunty Flo leaned over and whispered a well oiled secret in her ear, "Toby's working in Leonora in one of those big mines. He was living with a girl from South Australia. They had two kids, a boy named Benjiman and a girl called Lisa. Boy, I think three, and little girl, well she little one. Look like Tomby too."

"But, Aunty."

"Shhh, let me finish, girl," said Aunty Flo, who knew she was going to get a lot of questions flung at her. "Anyway, welfare came around before da funeral. I was talking to him on da phone. He wanted to come down, I said no. He asked how you getting on. I say you trying to be okay."

"Aunty, you said he was living with a woman from South Australia. What happened?"

"Well, she took off and left him. Took the kids with her. He on his own now."

Typical fuckin' Toby, she thought. Doesn't want to be cooped up, wants to be a feather blowin' in the wind.

"You listenin' to me, girl?" said Aunty Flo in a cross manner. The old lady was about to play the most important role of Brenda's life.

"Uhh, yeah Aunty," she said, nodding her head.

"I'm gonna tell you something now, girl. My cuzzin, Eunice, is comin' up to stay with me for a while. That's Toby's Aunty, too. Me and her used to be in Moore River Settlement together. She more like a sister to me. I never tell anybody 'bout dis. Not even Toby. Aunty Eunice know."

"Reason I tell you," she went on, "As a young woman I was madly in love with a young man from the Kimberley. He managed to escape one night, but before he did, he begged and begged me to go with him, but I was afraid of the superintendent. I watched my heart disappear into the darkness. I never found out what happened to him, I let him slip through my hands. I cried and cried for weeks after that. But nothing. What I wanna say, girl, is for you to go and look for Toby. Go, girl, go!"

At those words, Brenda grabbed the old lady. Hugging and crying, she whispered his name, "Toby, Toby, Toby."

Wiping her eyes and clearing her throat, Aunty Flo whispered in her ear, "Me and Aunty Eunice will look after the kids."

Six

Aunty Flo

Flo was sitting on the step of the verandah enjoying the warm sun. She and Brenda had just come from the church and she was in deep thought.

Eight months now, since that poor boy bin killed. Why couldn't Eunice come up? I know Brenda wanna go see Toby. Poor girl, cry when she hear his voice on da phone, thought Flo. She let her cardigan slip from her shoulders. It was a pleasant day. The sun was most gentle to her skin, sending the rivers of her blood gently flowing through her veins. Looking up, she noticed a car approaching with a black hand thrust out of the window, waving at her.

"No, can't be! 'Course is her," Flo gasped, her heart beating joyously as she got up to greet the vehicle.

Getting closer, Eunice stuck her head out of the window and yelled, "Flo, you old mare; is me. Your cuzzin, Eunice." Then the car stopped. The two old ladies were in each other's arms, hugging and crying. Flo untangled their embrace.

"Eunice. Oh, Eunice, you old . . . " Wiping away the tears and remembering she had just come from church, Flo didn't say what she wanted to say. She was afraid to upset the Lord.

"How you bin, Sis?" she asked, giving Eunice a good looking over. Sober, praise the Lord, she thought.

"Me, I bin solid. Dem old buntji mans still chasin me 'round down dere," was Eunice's cheeky reply. She knew full well what Flo's response would be.

"Choo. You got no shame. You think you young yorgah. Not anymore. You like me – old now." (It was the stern reply Eunice had expected.) Flo looked at the car. "Who dem Nyoongars?"

"My friends, dem big shot Nyoongars. Work in a big place in Perth somewhere," laughed Eunice, feeling very smug and possessive.

"Call 'em in for tea," suggested Flo.

"Hey, you two, wanna cuppa tea?" called Eunice.

Two well-dressed Aboriginal men got out, came over to Flo and introduced themselves.

"My name is Brannigan, Mrs . . . ?" Shaking her hand.

"Call me Aunty Flo," came her quick reply.

"Name's Charles," said the other one, doing

likewise, was told likewise. They declined the offered tea, saying they had to get back to Perth to their duties.

"What youse do?" asked Flo suspiciously.

Brannigan told her he and Charles worked for the Bandyup Women's Prison, looking after the welfare of the Aboriginal women who had just got out of there.

"What!" shrieked Flo, looking at Eunice for an explanation. She, in turn, doubled up in fits of laughter, and told her to get in contact with either Brannigan or Charles if her pension cheque was held up. They would get in contact with Social Security.

"Bye, then," they said, heading towards the car.

Watching it disappear out of sight, Flo turned to Eunice, who was still trying to control her laughter. Flo, too, burst out laughing, "Oh Eunice, you madda danna dawg with his ring on fire," then added, "Choo, you make me say silly things. Forgive me, Lord," she whispered.

That got both of them laughing again as they walked arm in arm to the house. Flo whispered to Eunice, "Be quiet, little one sleep." She guided Eunice into the kitchen, put on the kettle and tried hard not to laugh at her old cousin. "Why you bin jail for? And no lies." Eunice was getting a grip on herself, gave out a nasty cough, grimaced in pain and cleared her throat.

"You right, cuzz?" asked Flo, rushing around to her.

"Yeah, um right," she said, starting to look like Eunice again. "Just a sore throat."

Flo was concerned. She knew that that was no ordinary cough you get from colds or sore throats.

"Well, it was like dis, cuzz," with a twinkle and a smile, Eunice took Flo back to the last few remaining warm evenings that were left in the parks of Perth, before they were swallowed up by the approaching cold autumn winds.

"Anyway, cuzz, it was getting dark. Dis ol' wat-jella man pulled up in his flash car. Gawd, I was crook, had the shakes real bad . . . "

"Why you bring in the Lord's name for, alla time. He never say anything bad to you," scowled Flo.

"If He come to me, you know what I say to Him? Lord, get me a bottle of wine," was Eunice's cheeky reply.

"That Moore River Settlement make you silly," returned Flo.

"Anyway," Eunice continued, "he pulled up. I jumped in. He took me to a pub and got a bottle of wine. He pulled in some dark street, never min' how dark, I just wanna charge. Hey, you listenin?" growled Eunice.

"Yeah, 'course um listening," said Flo, expecting the full dirty story to come out of that old mouth. I think um gonna try and block my mind, thought Flo.

"Anyway, while I was drinkin,' he started to pull his fly down and pull his . . . "

"Aunty Eunice!" a shrill cry came, cutting the

sentence off and penetrating into Flo's partly blocked mind.

"When you come?" called Brenda, hugging Eunice.

Praise the Lord, thought Flo, if it wasn't for Brenda, she would've told me all the rest.

Hugging and crying, Eunice said to Brenda, "Um sad to hear 'bout dat man of yours. Aunty Flo told me all."

"Oh, Aunty, I don't know what to do," said Brenda, "I wanted to leave him, but dis happen."

"Never mind, girl. You listen to your heart. If He say you gotta go, you gotta go, girl," said Eunice.

Praise da Lord for dat. Is dis da same Eunice talkin? The same Eunice who is like wind blowin' from park to park, thought Flo.

"Let's have a cuppa tea," she said, making towards the stove. "Go and check on little one." Flo felt pleased with her niece. Brenda came back with Gina, who was still yawning. Sitting, she said to Gina, "Look, bub, Nanna Eunice here."

"She purty lookin' little yorgah, dis one," said Eunice, as Brenda passed Gina to her.

"Tea here," said Flo, giving Eunice and Brenda theirs and settling down to have her own. The three women talked for an hour or more. The two older women managed always to avoid the main issue, always choosing their words very carefully, knowing that Brenda didn't want to talk about that night.

Uncle Jacko walked in, swivelling his hips and

saying to Eunice, "Where my black snake is? Come here an wrap yourself all over me."

"Don't talk like dat here, Jacko. If you come here talkin like dat, you can get out," ordered Flo.

Uncle Jacko was too busy hugging Eunice to bother about her. But then, turning to Flo, he said with a toothless grin, "Look, Florence, when ol' Brickwall Jackson come to 'is ol' yorgah, no Bible's gunna stop 'im."

"How you know um here, Brickwall Jackson?" said Eunice, edging out Flo, who was inclined to stop all this nonsense talk.

"Well," he said, pulling himself into a gentlemanly composure only reserved for royalty, magistrates and justices of the peace in this little bush town, "I had dis dream you was a lady snake and I was the man snake, you see? Dis kookaburra swooped down, was ready to take you away, but I came through the grass and bit him on the ring. Instead of that kookaburra flying away laughing, poor thing flew away crying. Das when I know you was here." They all cracked up laughing; even Flo's no-nonsense approach was shattered.

The Nyoongar community started their ritual coming in to see Eunice. They all yarned with her, complimenting how the dye in her hair made her look so much younger than seventy odd years or more, which made her giggle, and caused Flo to get into a huff. She think she movie star now, thought Flo.

But, deep down, Eunice knew that it wouldn't be too long for her to meet with the spirits of her ancestors. Tell um later, she thought. The crowd slowly disappeared. Only Jacko had hung on or clowned around although the taste of grape juice was beckoning him.

"Well, I better be going now. I got a price lined up," he kissed Eunice on the cheek and headed for the door, leaving Flo, Eunice, Brenda and her three kids, all together as family. Flo, being the elder spokesperson, decided right there and then to, as Eunice would say, put all da cards on da table.

Brenda told Flo and Eunice that the two boys were taken care of because Aunty Phyllis would look after them. "I'll send money down to her." She said she was able to handle Gina, whom she would like with her. She got up and took little one to the bathroom. Eunice decided to lay down and have a rest.

Flo's mind went back to the days of Moore River Settlement. Poor Eunice, she thought, as she sat alone, always getting flogged alla time for nothin, jus' cause she was darker dan all of us. Those superintendents, dey was bad to us black-fellas.

She still remembered her first love, who had disappeared into the night. Kenny from Kimberley, dey called 'im. But he probably dead now. I shoulda run away with 'im.

She remembered the puffy red face of the superintendent looking at her and saying, just before she left there, "Now, Florence, you can go out to work now. You're a big girl also you are a fair skin girl, you're not black."

"Yes, sir," Flo had said, barely a whisper.

"What I am saying is for you to marry a white man. You'll have a roof over your head, a warm bed and have food in your cupboards and, also, your children will be white. Hopefully your race will be wiped out through your children. Never marry a black man. You will always be on a reserve. Living in a humpy in filth and the authorities can shoot him whenever they like. You understand me, girl?" Puffy Face screamed at her, his blood vessels practically popping out.

Yeah, she thought, I did that and may the Lord forgive me.

Her husband had taken his frustrations out on Flo because his white mates used to ridicule him for being married to a gin. His white community didn't want to know him, and the Nyoongars from on the reserve sympathised with Flo for being married to a white man. The only way he could vent his anger was with his fists and scathing remarks about her people. Flo's fragile body had withstood all the punishment that was bestowed upon her.

When he was killed in an accident at work, Flo thought it was the Lord's way of getting rid of the rubbish. "Yes, Mr Red Puffy Face, wherever you are, I did marry him for a warm bed, a house and food. Not love. Like you said, I didn't wanna live in a humpy, on a reserve with all that love and laughter around," she said to herself.

Her people had welcomed her back with open

arms, shared her sorrows and looked after her fragile body, bringing it back to health and happiness by blackfella way only.

These mob I tell off, they know I don't mean it. Long as I got my church and the Lord, um happy. She wiped away the tears that streamed down her face.

"What you cryin for, Aunty?" Brenda said suddenly. "I'll get Toby to ring up, you know that."

"Don't frighten me, girl," said Flo, grabbing for her chest, "I was just thinkin' 'bout long time ago." She told Brenda what happened at Moore River Settlement.

"Well, I'm off. I think Aunty Phyllis' car comin' now," said Brenda, peeking through the curtains.

"Okay, den, girl. Look after little one and let me know what you and Toby gonna do. Ring up welfare. Me and Aunty Eunice go for walk there," she said, as she was hugging Brenda and giving Gina a big kiss.

After Brenda had gone, Flo tidied up the kitchen and had a cup of tea. She then decided to go to bed, first checking on her old cuzz.

"You right, cuzz?" whispered Flo.

"Yeah, um right, cuzz," replied Eunice hoarsely.

Settling into bed, Flo thought of Eunice. That coughing was trying to tell me somethin.' I know she not well. Um gunna ask her first thing in the morning, Flo decided as she drifted into a thoughtless sleep.

The figures were so real in Flo's dreams. It was

played right before her eyes and she could not do a thing about it. As a matter of fact, she was obeying her cuzz's command, "I come back to die. Nothink you can do about it. Doctors told me before I come up here but before that, our old Grandmother Florence, your namesake, tol' me to come to you and you know she bin dead for a long time. I got cancer in the throat. I go back to room now, they come for me."

She could see Eunice wave to her and disappear from her sight. Again, in her dreams, she can see two old warriors walk into Eunice's room and sit down on the floor by her bed. They begin to hum a mournful note.

"No!" screams Flo, "I 'member you two warriors in Moore River Settlement. You two were old fellas when I was a little girl. Don't let my old cuzz die"

No words come out of her mouth. She is screaming in her mind. As the mournful note continues, their claps are turning to sorrow. The dream disappears as it came. So quickly, as sunlight casts its sorrowful rays over the house.

Stirring, Flo got up and had a cup of tea. No birds dis mornin', she thought, I know why.

Uncle Jacko walked in, grabbed Flo and said, "I know she gone. Birds all quiet. No breeze, sun feels cold dis mornin'. You bin in room yet?"

"No," said Flo in barely a whisper. "When the birds start singin' and the sun warms up, das when I go in for a look."

Jacko put his head down and started to hum

that same mournful note. Flo burst out crying, letting the tears flow free, forming a puddle at her feet.

"Ni. Ni. Listen," Jacko said quietly. The birds started to chirp slowly at first, then they picked up the tempo, as the sun burst into the room.

"I look, see now," said Flo.

"I get um amb'lence now," whispered Jacko, about to leave the room.

"You know, Jacko," she said, stopping him in his tracks. "We must always put our culture first. We gotta put it back into our children. I know those missionaries tried their best. I got dis feelin' dat our ancestors are even teachin' God our culture."

After those words from Flo, a real strong Christian lady, he was, for a moment, speechless.

Then Jacko said, "Poor Eunice, make you realise our own time will come soon enough. I'll miss my ol' black snake," and he walked out of the house.

Seven

Mary[*]

It was getting late. Mary, who was ten, was crying on the street corner. She didn't want to go back home.

I'd rather be a street kid than be a slave for Mummy and Daddy, while they carry on drinking with all our relations. I like to play with my friends' dolls, instead of looking after my little brother and sister all the time. I wish they would give up drinking and kick those other Nyoongars out who come around with their bottles, she thought between sobs.

"Why are you crying, my dear?"

Mary looked up and saw a kind face looking down at her, with her arms outstretched. Mary went into those arms and sobbed.

*(*To My Sister, Mary)*

"Now, now," said the kind old lady, "Tell me, what's the matter," holding her and patting her head.

Mary told her all. The kindly old lady, Sister Bernadine, suggested Mary come home to her place to have a meal, spend the night and pray for Mummy and Daddy. Sister Bernadine promised to take her back in the morning.

The next morning, Sister Bernadine took her back and all the family was pleased to see Mary. Her mother told her about the dream she had had that night.

She said that in her dream, Mary was playing on the edge of a cliff. She was running to bring Mary back from there when she stumbled and fell, waking herself up.

She hugged Mary, told her that Mummy and Daddy weren't going to drink any more, or let their relations come around with their bottles. They were all going to live as a family, helping each other.

Mary looked at the kindly old nun, who was wiping a tear from her eye and saying, "God will help those who seek him."

Eight

The Best Night Of My Life!

The stillness of the warm, tropical North Queensland night was shattered by the vehement spitting of machine gun fire. An RAAF F111 flew overhead almost skimming the trees and giving the friendly force (which was us, the Royal Australian Army) a backburn. The backburn was a flame more than 200 metres long, let out of the F111's rear end by the pilot and turned the inky blackness of the night brighter than the day itself.

This was not a real battle, but a battle between two friendly countries (Australia and Malaya) which had been orchestrated by the United Nations. The Malayans, who were on an exchange agreement, were at that time in conflict with their own rebel soldiers. When we were demonstrating how easy it was to walk into an ambush, I thought to myself, thank God, this is not the real thing.

I was conversing with a couple of Malayan soldiers when we overheard voices coming from the radio. I didn't get the beginning of the conversation, but what I picked up bewildered us all. Our Commanding Officer, from about 200 kilometres away, ordered us to hastily prepare a heli-pad on a flat piece of ground.

Both friendly countries laboriously endured the task of preparing the heli-pad. We lit small fires around the pad and everything was set up. Within minutes we heard the helicopter choppering away in the distance, like a giant eagle about to swoop down on its prey. It hovered above us with the lights on, the undercarriage lit up, before it slowly descended.

What happened next was even more bewildering. The company sergeant, after talking to the pilot, came over to me and snapped. "Private Yallup, get your gear. You're going back."

"Yes, Sir," I said, coming to attention and not daring to question an order.

I put on my gear in the chopper and strapped myself in. We took off. It was eerie flying in the inky blackness of the night. All sorts of questions were going through my mind. I felt as though I was being swallowed up by the universe. The swishing of the rotor blades of the chopper stripped the humidity from around us. Peering onto the darkness, I tried to catch a glimpse of man-made light.

After about an hour, the pilot grabbed my attention and pointed to the south. I could see what I'd been looking for – a band of flickering lights away in the distance. The lights seemed to me to be dancing in time with the helicopter's motor.

It was a relief to approach the lights of Laverrack Barracks in Townsville, where the battalion of the 2nd/4th was based. Like an eagle with tired wings, we practically fell out of the sky, landing with a bump on the parade ground.

Grabbing my gear, I gave a thumbs-up to the pilot and dashed to a waiting landrover which took me to the guardhouse. Running into the guardhouse, I was confronted by the Commanding Officer. On seeing him I came quickly to attention. I saluted and at the same time said, "Sir!".

"Private Yallup," he said, "Your wife is about to give birth. I have relieved you of your duties so that you could be with your wife. Sign in your weapon and your gear. A rover will take you in, best of luck."

"Yes, Sir, thank you, Sir," I replied, in a clear, crisp voice.

Before long, I was in the hospital where I was met by a sister, who ushered me into the theatre. There, before my eyes, a near-perfect miracle was happening.

Holding this little bundle of joy, I felt tears of happiness and joy flowing and, above all, relief that she was screaming her lungs out.

That, to me, was the best night of my life.

Nine

Granny Daisy

I remember Granny Daisy. Some say she belonged to the devil's clan, others say she belonged to the holy spirits of our ancestors who gave her incredible powers. But I know her powers were for the good. She rewarded good with good and bad with bad.

Old Granny Daisy lived at the back of the reserve in a tin humpy. She was an old Wongi woman. They say she was 110 when she died, some say older. But how can they say she died when they couldn't find her body.

All the Wongi people moved away from the reserve into the edges of town, but Granny Daisy, no way. She was a part of the bush like the trees, scrubs, rocks and the soil. I, myself, have seen her blend so well into the vegetation that you don't see her until she growls at you, sending shivers down your spine. Not an angry growl, but a growl to let you know she was there.

*

My father came running into the house shouting to Mother, "Topsy, Topsy, Granny Daisy's humpy is burning down and they think she's in it."

I heard Mum say, "Quick, Kingie, do something." I didn't wait for Dad's reply, I was out of the house and going as fast as my twelve year old feet could move, through a vacant lot, down an alley and by a church. As I got close to the church, I slowed down to a walk, wondering whether to go in or not. Shall I go in and pray to God and ask him to save Granny Daisy? Naw, I thought, She has great powers of her own. I'm sure no fire could hurt her, so I gathered speed again and got to the top of the hill overlooking the reserve. I could see smoke and flames all over the bushes where she once had her humpy. I took off for a down hill run and in no time I was there.

People were running around and pumping water on the flames. As I got closer I felt the heat on my face and took a step back. Nothing left, only burning rubble that was once a neat humpy. I ran to a man who was trying to douse the flames with water. "Where's Granny Daisy, is she among all that rubble?"

"We wouldn't know till we put out the flames and the ashes have cooled down," said the man, "I suggest you keep out of the way, go on, off you go." By this time most of the Wongi people had gathered around talking amongst themselves. My dad was there so I sauntered over towards him. My father was a Nyoongar and my mother a Wongi. It turned out my grandmother was a full blood and my grandfather was a white man. So being half-caste, my mother was taken away by the Native Affairs when she was a young girl and was just coming to terms with the dark blood flowing through her veins.

My mother and father never mastered the Wongi language, only a few words here and there to communicate with our Wongi people, who, in turn, never bothered about the English language. Words mainly used were flour, tea and sugar. After learning these words, why bother about the English language?

My father called out, "Benji, get out of the way or you'll get yourself run over. And how did you get here?" he asked

"I ran all the way here," I said, feeling all grown up. I left Dad and went over to the group of boys I knocked around with. Scraper, Teddie, Bullit, MP, Warra and Cosmo were standing looking very solemn. All these boys were in my age group except Scraper, who was a couple of years older than us lot. He thought he was Bruce Lee, Rambo and Charlie Pride all rolled into one. Even though we were younger than Scraper, we always seemed to have it over him. Maybe his brain was a bit slow to absorb whatever was told to him, but we voted him our leader.

"Hello, Scraper," I said, it was short for 'sky-scraper'.

"Hi there, Benji boy," he said, "Poor old Granny Daisy haven't got her powers to get out of this one."

"Yeah, I think she's finished," said Bullit, getting out of the smoke.

"I don't know so much," said Cosmo, "I seen her pick up a tiger snake in her humpy and pat him on the head and say, 'Off you go, boy.' Didn't we, Benji?"

"I seen her too, once, giving her dugite a drink of water," said Teddie.

"Maybe she turned herself into a snake and just slithered away before it got too hot for her," said MP.

"Or into a crow and flew away," said Warra, looking up to the trees.

"Look, you boys, stop talking silly," said Scraper, putting on the number one act. "I don't think anyone can live through that. I know she has great powers, but . . . " he looked a little uncertain, "No, I don't think so."

"Let's get closer, only tins and ashes left," said MP. With a bit of consideration we edged our way forward, then, realizing he was our leader, Scraper said, "Hang on, you boys, did I say we can go and have a closer look?"

"Look, Scraper, we're here now so what's the use?" I said.

"Yeah, yeah," we all said without meaning.

Everything was under control now so we looked around to see if anything there resembled Granny Daisy, hoping and praying that she wasn't amongst all that rubble. A big policeman came over towards us and said, "Come on, Scraper, get your gang out of here." Everyone knew Scraper because of his height, nose and his great big feet, not necessarily in that order.

"I wouldn't like you boys around when we sift through all this rubble." said the policeman. "Go to your parents, I've explained everything to them."

We looked around to our dads who were waving us to them. When we got there, Uncle Leroy, who is Scraper's dad, told us that children are not allowed when they sift through the rubble.

"Aw, gee, Dad, I'm nearly fifteen, these kids here can go home, I'll wait with you," said Scraper.

"Off you go, Leroy."

That was Scraper's real name and Uncle Leroy never called Scraper that unless he was being challenged. Scraper soon got the message.

"Okay, Dad," he said and ran to catch us up.

As he drew abreast with us, MP said, "Thanks for sticking up for us, Scraper."

"That's okay, anytime, koord," he said.

"What MP means, is that you said, 'Send these kids home.' You're not much older than us, sometimes I wonder why you are our leader," said Teddie.

"I am your leader. Anyone say otherwise, I'll

make 'em piss," Scraper dropped into a kung fu stance.

"Aw, come on, Scraper, forget about it," said Warra.

"You tell that to this little black grasshopper," said Scraper doing a kung fu kick towards Teddie who, along with the rest of us, burst out laughing.

"Hey, don't say I'm good as Bruce Lee," said Scraper.

"Better," said Cosmo, trying to stop himself from laughing.

"Even Bruce Lee got nothing on you, koord," said Bullit.

But we all knew what he looked like – a giant squid floundering around on the Great Gibson Desert. Better change the subject, I thought, or we'll piss ourselves laughing.

"I wonder if Granny Daisy is under all that rubble?" I said.

"Yeah," said Teddie, forgetting about Scraper's silly antics.

"Remember the time we all went to the reserve to play cowboys and Indians?" said Warra.

"Sure do," said Bullit, shivering in the warm afternoon sun.

"I'll never forget," said MP.

*

We had all decided to go to the reserve for a game on a warm summer's evening, so we split into our two groups. It was Scraper, MP, Bullit and Cosmo who always played the cowboys whilst Teddie, Warra and me played the Indians. Warra always argued with Scraper about the extra boy. Scraper always came up with the brilliant reply of, “Look Warra, you are a better shot than all of us so I need the extra one.”

Warra, grinning from ear to ear and his pearly white teeth glistening in his dusky face, was a sight to see agreeing with Scraper saying, “Yeah, you can have the extra cowboy, we’ll be right,” while lifting up the stick in his hand and pretending to blow Scraper’s knee caps off from under him. Imagine Warra being a better shot than the lot of us with a stick gun. Well, I thought, if these two ever had an I.Q. test, I would hate to pick a winner.

We started playing away from Granny Daisy’s humpy. We were so engrossed with our game that we weren’t aware that we had managed to drift towards her humpy until we heard this moaning and groaning coming from within the humpy. It switched to a real sad wailing noise, then to a rasping, screeching sound like someone was trying to saw through bones with a blunt saw. It was weird and we’d heard some weird noises before, like when all the tribe got together, but this wasn’t human. That was the fastest treaty ever signed by the cowboys and Indians as we all huddled together listening to those unnatural sounds. We didn’t know whether to run or stay put. Of course, Scraper, with his long legs, would make it home first but, no way was he going to move from us; he had a vice-like grip on Teddie's and my arms.

"What shall we do, Scraper?" said Cosmo, looking at the track that lead to town.

"Keep your voice down," whispered Teddie

"Let's have a closer look," whispered Warra, not too convincingly.

"Shhh," I whispered, "listen." Abruptly it stopped. We stood frozen looking at the humpy.

It was more through fear than courage that we moved closer to the humpy. We shouted at the top of our voices, "Granny Daisy, you alright?" Then came a sound like someone was breaking sticks to our left. That was the last straw! We bolted back towards town, stumbling, crying, falling over one another, swearing, cursing and praying for help. We were just like a big, black cloud coming towards town and there was a sigh of relief as the lights came into view as we all hit town together.

We stood under a street light panting. Scraper got us all to stand around him in a circle as he raised his arms and eyes to the heavens and said, "May the spirits of our ancestors look over and protect us while we can see the trees, rocks, animals, feel the wind on our faces and above all, feel the soil under our bare feet, amen." We all said 'amen' together and went our separate ways.

I've often thought of those noises at night while waiting for sleep. Warra said it was her pet tiger snake giving birth to her baby snakes. Cosmo said it was her living spirit trying to contact the dead. MP said it was the white spirits screaming out in hell and asking Granny Daisy's forgiveness for all the wrong doings that were done to her when she was a young girl. I tend to lean towards MP's suggestion as it seemed to have more foundation.

*

Many times I have eavesdropped on old Uncle Henry telling Dad about Granny Daisy. He was a boy when she was a young woman. His grandfather told him many years ago how she was brutally raped, bashed and tied naked to a tree by a group of watjellas and used whenever they wanted her. Another time three prospectors came upon Granny Daisy, her mother, father and little sister, who was about thirteen at that time. They killed her father by slitting his throat, then proceeded to do the most evil things to the three females before slitting her mother's and sister's throats in front of Granny Daisy. Then they got the blood and smeared it all over her bruised and battered body. They dragged a whimpering Granny Daisy to a bull-ants' nest and staked her over it, leaving her for the bull-ants to pick away at her living flesh, before they went on their merry way, so full of laughter, so full of courage.

I think it was then, from the impressions of Uncle Henry, that Grannv Daisy became aware that she had great powers. Whilst immobile, she began to hum a mournful tune to her holy ancestors. Then she stopped and, not daring to breathe, she felt a million or more tiny feet trample all over her, investigating every part of her body but not one bit her. As if commanded by the spirits above, big black clouds gathered overhead and burst open upon her. As the rain came down the bull-ants scampered back to the safety of their nest.

Granny Daisy lay there on her back feeling the rain falling on her, she still had that tingling sensation of the bull-ants that had corroboreed all over her body. She must have dozed off because when she awoke the sun was shining and the ground around her was saturated. The stakes were easily pulled out by moving her arms and legs. She undid the ropes around her arms and legs and got up very slowly at first, then gingerly walked around feeling to see if any bones were broken. "No, none at all," she sobbed.

She then proceeded to dig a shallow grave to bury her loved ones, sobbing silently as she laboriously put them in and covered them with the soil while vowing vengeance on those murderers. She lay sobbing by her family's grave, not aware that a tiger snake was moving gracefully towards her, along with a dugite and three little ones, a dingo and a rabbit. Above in a tree a crow was cawing out aloud.

The tiger snake slowly slithered over her body trying to comfort her and it was then she became aware of all the other animals. What a strange combination of animals, she thought, this can't be real! The rabbit hopped over the dugite to rub his soft, furry body against her hip as if to say we are all your friends. The dingo came over to lick her face as the dugite and her babies coiled themselves around her legs. The crow came and landed next to her with its head hanging to one side, slowly walking towards her. She reached out and patted its head, saying softly, "I am alive, my black friend, you know how bad you are treated when you are black." As if he understood, the crow cawed three times, then flew to the highest branch as if to become a sentry to his friends below.

Yes, old Unle Henry had a lot of stories to tell about Granny Daisy as told to him by his grandparents. Stories passed down by tribal elders to keep the Wongi law in today's society. But with alcohol and drugs dominating the younger generation and these black religious leaders confusing people, our tribal customs are slowly dying.

Another time, I remember Mum had made a big damper and she asked me to take a piece to Granny Daisy. Cosmo, who was playing with me at the time, grabbed the damper and we went up to see her. Everything was quiet as we approached her humpy. Knocking on the side of the tin wall I called out, "Granny Daisy, Mum sent you a piece of damper."

"Come in, boys," she called in broken English. Inside we noticed a chair, table and the bed which she was sitting on. She looked so frail sitting there, yet there was a blue aura just above her head.

Cosmo bumped me and whispered, "She is truly a

holy woman."

"You boys been good to Granny Daisy, put it on the table," she said, snapping us back to reality.

"Getting warm for you, Granny Daisy?" asked Cosmo.

"Yeah, boy, getting warm now, won't be long before the animals come out for water. Who sent this?" she asked.

"Aunty Topsy, Benjamin's mum," Cosmo told her.

"Ahh, she been a good girl to me that one. Don't move," she said in a commanding voice, as she grabbed her walking stick and hobbled towards us. At first we thought she was going to hit us with her stick, but she bent down and picked up a snake right at our feet. Well, I reckon our healthy twelve year old hearts stopped beating for a whole minute. She patted its head, stroked its body then put it down and said, "Go on, get, they are my blood, too," before settling down on the bed.

"We'd better be going," I said, making towards the door, my legs still shaking.

"Listen, boys, when you go back, walk by the pipe, you will see a rock shining in the sun. Pick it up and take it home to your dad," she said.

"Is it gold?" asked Cosmo.

"Just do as you're told," she said.

"Bye, Granny Daisy," we called as we walked out into the sunlight. I said to Cosmo, "You go to the top end of the pipe and I'll go down over here," pointing to the bottom end.

"Yeah, okay," he said walking off.

I walked slowly along the pipe looking down, my heart beating in anticipation for I knew what she was talking about was gold. But how could gold be here, further out maybe, but miners have prospected this ground a million times over and have found nothing.

"To all the beautiful spirits of my ancestors!" I heard Cosmo call out.

It didn't take me long to make up the space between us.

"I can't believe it!" I shouted, looking down. Cosmo was a full blood and I wasn't far behind him, but at that moment I'm sure we turned white, whiter than Snow White and the Seven Dwarves all put together. For there on the ground, shining in the sun, was a lump of gold in the shape of a dingo's head. It wasn't in the ground but on top, as though it was put there for us.

I bent down slowly and reached for it. As I picked it up and rubbed the palm of my hand over it, I'm sure it was breathing. This rock is alive, I thought.

"Here, feel this," I said to Cosmo passing the gold over.

He put his hands out very slowly as if afraid to touch it. This rock was the size of a clenched fist, the weight must be about ten kilos.

Cosmo grabbed the rock and rubbed his hand over it, saying, "Hey, this rock seems to be breathing, it's alive." Then, rubbing his hands all over his chest, added, "I'm sure it has a spirit of its own."

Take your shirt off and wrap it up," I said. We looked towards Granny Daisy's humpy. She was standing at the door with her walking stick supporting her and her free hand waving us to get along home. It didn't take us long to get our skinny legs pounding the red soil under our bare feet as we ran to the house.

"Hey, slow down, you two," said Mum, who was sitting in the lounge.

"Look, Mum, what we found!" I said, whilst Cosmo put it on the coffee table in front of her.

Mum didn't seem surprised, just asked, "Did Granny Daisy have anything to do with this?"

"She told us where to find it," said Cosmo.

"Go and get your Dad, he's out the back," she said to me.

I rushed out back and called Dad to the lounge. He wasn't too surprised at the great lump of gold sitting on the coffee table. Dad looked at Mum and sat down, telling me and Cosmo to sit down too, and put our eyes back in their sockets. After gaining some composure, we sat down.

"I'll take it to the gold buyers tomorrow, we should get about $5,000 or more for this.

"That's a lot of money," I said, bumping Cosmo with my elbow.

"Of course, I got to split it with the rest of the community," said Dad, reaching out to touch it then pulling his hand back.

"You feel it, too, Uncle Kingie?" said Cosmo.

"I sure did," said Dad, expecting the rock to

start talking.

Mum, who was sitting quietly by Dad, smiled and asked, "Did you feel as though you picked up a living rock?"

"Yeah, Mum, like it was breathing, unna, Cosmo?"

"Yeah, Aunty Topsy, it was funny, you know what I mean?" he asked.

"Yes, Cosmo, I understand, everything has a spirit of its own. The rock's spirit will depart after all the fondling it will be put through."

"Dad, you said we'll get $5,000 or more, can we keep it all? We can give some to Cosmo and his family. No one will know," I said eagerly.

"Granny Daisy will know, she wants black-fellas to be caring and sharing, not against each other. When they get a guts full of plonk they just want to kill each other, that's bad," said Dad.

"Uncle Kingie, can I ask you a question I've always wanted to ask Dad but was afraid to, but you, being a Nyoongar and not a Wongi, might be able to help me."

"I'll try the best I can," said Dad to Cosmo.

"Was Granny Daisy born like us, or was she born like Jesus, you know, like the angels coming down and telling her mother that she was going to have a holy baby and her name was going to be Daisy?"

"No, Cosmo," said Dad, smiling, "she was born just like you and me, Benji and Aunt Topsy here, but who knows . . . "

"I'll tell youse a story about Granny Daisy and her powers," said Dad. Cosmo and I settled in the seat while Mum got up to make Dad a cup of tea.

"I just got up here from Perth, I didn't know your mother then, anyway, it didn't take me long to get a job here on one of the mines. We also had a lot of young white blokes up here working. It was one pay day, we were all in the pub having a beer. These young blokes were bragging about how they used to give the cops a hard time with their high-powered cars in Perth. The cops never caught them, or so they say, but they had a skinful of booze and one of the blokes had a high-powered GT1. I think they wanted some kicks. One idiot said, 'Hey, there's an old coon woman who lives in the bush on her own, let's go and stir her up'."

"The rotten mongrels," I said, hitting my fist into the palm of my hand.

"They gotta be rotten," said Cosmo, seething.

"Hang on, let me finish," said Dad, just as Mum came in with the tea and sat down. "Now where was I?" said Dad, "Yeah, about five of them jumped into the car and that car was fairly grumbling with power when it took off. They must have been gone for three hours or more when the sergeant and constable walked in. Both seemed in a state of shock. They were deathly white as they walked up to the bar, ordered a double whisky each and drank it straight down. By this time all the drinkers had gathered around. 'Right,' said the Sarge, as his colour came back to him, 'you know those five young blokes who were drinking here earlier on? Well, they've had a bad accident just down from Daisy's humpy. God, it was sickening, the worst accident I've ever seen.

The driver and the bloke in front were decapitated. The car was practically pushed under a pipe. You could see the skid marks around old Daisy's humpy, but what we can't get over was that the track leading back to town was on their right, but they took the left turn straight through the reserve and smack, straight under the pipe. Their tracks suggested they were completely out of control before going under the pipe.'

'What happened to the three at the back?' asked the barman.

'They're dead too,' said the Sarge, 'it's so queer that their faces and throats were twisted up with fear. Puncture marks all over their faces and throats. Seemed like a lot of snakes crawled in and bit them after the accident.'

'Looks to me as if the snakes were in the car before they actually hit the pipe judging from the looks on their faces. So full of fear it's unnatural,' said the constable, shaking his head.

'Come on, Ken,' said the Sarge to his offsider, 'let's get back to the station. The boys from Perth should be up on the next flight, they might find a little more than we did. We've done all we can, notified their parents, so it's up to the blokes from Perth,' as they walked out, still shaking their heads."

"Did the cops from Perth find anything new

from what Sarge said?" asked Cosmo.

"No, I don't think so, they just put it down as too much booze, lost control, just another number to the road toll, case closed," said Dad.

"I wonder what happened, I mean, really, really happened?" I asked.

"From what I can gather from Uncle Henry and Uncle Leroy, those young blokes spun around Granny Daisy's humpy a number of times. Yelling filth and calling her all the dirtiest names you can lay your tongue on. Then they parked in front of her place, got out of the car and started throwing empty stubbies at her humpy. One big fat mother snake slithered into the back of the car, instantly gave birth to a dozen or more little ones who in turn gave birth to more. So when they jumped back into the car, there were snakes everywhere. Uncle Henry reckons they were dead before hitting the pipe. By the way, there wasn't a snake found dead or alive in the car," said Dad, as an after thought.

"Wow, she sure is one powerful lady," I said.

"Another time, when she was a young woman, according to Uncle Henry," said Dad, "it was Granny Daisy, her little sister, her mother and father. When three prospectors came upon their camp, they terrorised the family killing the father, the mother and the little sister, then staked Granny Daisy to a bull-ants' nest and leaving her to die. As the men rode off, big black clouds gathered overhead and within minutes, thunder and lightning cracked all around them then it poured with rain. As they huddled under a tree for cover, a bolt of lightning struck the tree where they stood, knocking the three men and their horses to the ground and into unconsciousness. As the men and their horses lay on the ground barely breathing, a flock of crows landed next to them. They started to pick their eyes out, then started on their broken skins. Along came a pack of dingoes who started to rip out their throats. With the aroma of fresh blood, fresh broken flesh hanging in the air, the other reptiles and creatures picked up the scent and helped to strip the men and beasts of their flesh.

The sergeant and his search party found them a couple of days later. They felt sick about it for weeks after. A few of the men from the search party ended up in a mad-house in Perth somewhere."

"She put that gold for you to find. Don't ask me how," said Dad.

*

As Scraper, Teddie, Cosmo, Bullit, MP, Warra and myself walked away from her burned down humpy, not one of us spoke. Our heads hung down in silence. All those memories going through our minds.

I don't know what it was, but something made us look up together at a big tree and high on a branch was a big crow. It looked down at us, cawed loudly three times, then flew away. Scraper spoke our thoughts out aloud when he shouted. “It’s Granny Daisy. She is still with us.” As the crow flew out of sight, we all shouted in one voice. “We love you, Granny Daisy. Please watch over us.”

We were the happiest mob of black kids that anyone ever saw as we ran for home.

Ten

The day before

"Gee, I'm crook, don't think I'll be able to wait 'til tomorra," said Jim.

"Yeah, me too, fuck dis, all dese Nyoongars are broke 'til tomorra and dese watjellas won't give anything 'til I pay my debts."

"Just have ta suffer 'til tomorra," said old Blue.

You see, it was very bad before pension day. All the Nyoongars were broke in this little wheat-belt community where they lived on one side of town and the watjellas lived on the other. The whites wanted to get right away from the drunken Nyoongars and also those Christian Nyoongars who were singing hymns and preaching to all who were game enough to listen. Those Christian Nyoongars had no say over those who drank and they also kept right away from them. The old drunken Nyoongar was able to get on with anyone in the town, mainly with the local sergeant of the police station, who was always helpful towards the Nyoongar community. For this he copped a lot of flack from the white side of town. Poor old Sarge was in a no-win situation.

The day before pension was hell; no money for a drink, food, the SEC was threatening to cut off the power, no gas, the welfare wouldn't give you any rations because the bloody government . . . bloody government gave only so much per family, most of the Nyoongars had blown their amount in less than no time.

"You know, if we were in Perth, we'd be able to get some tucker and a price for a bottle with all those welfare mob down there," said Jim.

"But we're not fuckin' down there so we just gotta suffer 'til tomorra," said Blue.

"Yeah, an' most of dese youn' Nyoongar blokes get cheques tomorra," said Jim.

Old Bluey and Jim were two old blokes who liked their drop of port whenever they had some money, which wasn't very often. Mainly it was pension days that they gave the port a good bashing, but today was a no no. Like old Blue said, he was up to his ears in debt. You see, old Bluey and Jim were reared up around this place. They didn't get much schooling because they had to go out and work. Most of the men folk on the reserve had to work to eat. There were no pensions in those days, no dole cheques. All the Nyoongars had to get out of town before 6.00 p.m. If they were good enough and if the Native Welfare saw fit, they might get their citizenship rights, which allowed them to buy their grog without being hassled by the publican or the law.

Life on the reserve was a happy one for old Bluey and Jim, while growing up with their respective brothers and sisters. Their fathers had built their homes out of discarded sheets of iron. When they were finished, their homes looked like modern day tin humpies. They had no electricity and the kids had to go to the pipe, which ran along in front of the reserve, for water, so bathing or taking a shower was a bonus whenever they could have one.

Old Bluey's father had a wireless in his camp and he always liked to keep in contact with the rest of the world around him. He knew King George and Robert Menzies were some sort of tribal leaders and, at night, Australia played England at cricket. Blue would lay down at night and listen to cricket with his father. He would often think, if this man Bradman could make one hundred runs or more at night, imagine what he'd make in daylight hours. Little did Bluey know it was daytime in England.

During the day, Blue's old man, along with Jim's father, would round up all the family and go out and work for the local farmer. It was clearing time and most of the virgin land not far from the reserve needed clearing. Bluey and Jim would always look forward to these outings because it was turned into a picnic by the kids. The mothers would take tea, sugar, milk and a bit of flour if they were lucky. Dad and the boys would take water and matches and the farmers would supply the axes and shovels.

Bluey, Jim, their uncles and cousins would prepare to start clearing the land while Bluey and Jim's old man, respectively, built a bough shed for the women folk, who helped to prepare the meals for the men. Some days the meals were very flash; roasted kangaroo, hot ashes damper with treacle followed by a big pannikin of hot white tea.

As old Bluey would say later on in life, "Dey were the bes' days ob my life." He would quite often tell Jim around a bottle of port, "Dis gub men' is gibbin' dese youn' fellas money to do nothin' today. Why don't dey gib dem some lan' an' make dese youn' fuckers work it, instead ob gibbin dem money for gerbah, or start dem in der own business."

Jim would say, "Yeah, but dese youn' people want to han' around der mothers and fathers all der libes, eben when dey are married with kids. If dey do make somethin' of demselves, all der mob will come around, cadging off dem, so you see, Blue, a black fellas got a hard act to follow. He don' wanna upset his uncles, aunties, brothers or sisters, so he either gibs all his 'lations money or none at all. But if he don' gibs dem money and he dribes a fancy car, libes in a flash house, wears good clothes, he's a stuck-up black bastard. Yes, Blue, we were lucky to lib in da good old days, all together, happy, no family feuding."

Blue and Jim would often go back to the past. Bluey was taught to shear by his Uncle Keith at the age of seventeen, got his citizenship rights at twenty five, came down with arthritis and had a chronic alcohol problem at forty five. He joined the Christian church to kick his habit, but it was easier to get a bottle of port than it was to hobble to church. He was finally pensioned off at fifty.

Leaving the reserve had been sad, his ties lay back in the soil. He crawled, played, slept, and made love to his beautiful wife, God rest her soul, but living in a state house with his wife and son was very depressing. His neighbours were all white. Old Blue remembered when he was a child running around naked and free in the bush. It was natural. He also remembered his grandmother telling him his father used to run naked through the bushes, playing amongst the wild flowers. But in town, his wife, Topsy, wouldn't let young Louie junior run naked, not in front of those white folks, never.

Old Bluey often thought of Mr Williams, the Native Welfare boss, saying, "Now Louie, Topsy, you are living in town. Try and live like these white people here. Keep some clothes on young Louie. Keep your house clean. Keep away from the pub. Don't let all your tribe come here and stay. Smile and say hello to your neighbours and you will become like these nice people here. I know you're a good shearer, try and save your money. I know you've got your citizenship rights, don't supply those other natives with grog or the police will get you three months for supplying. Now, you don't want to go to jail for three months, do you, leaving Topsy and Louie all alone?"

"You know, Jim, I reckon old Mr Williams thought he knew more about me than I did about myself," said old Blue, smiling to himself "Yeah, dey reckon he kicked da bucket a rich ol' man."

"Yeah, rich with black fellas' money," said Jim. Yes, Bluey and Jim worked all this land around here for the farmers, working from daylight to dusk. A bit of flour, tea, sugar, tobacco and ten bob was all they got, if they were lucky. All the root picking, hay carting, hay stooking, seeding, harvesting and whatever job was ready for them. Yeah, in those days, the farmers came right out to the reserve to pick up the Nyoongars and brought them home again. At the end of the day, the farmers' wives would give all the men a dozen eggs each and some meat, if the boss had done a killing, to take home to their families.

Once all the Nyoongars pooled their money together and bought an old jalopy. When work was scarce they would take off and go woolpicking, so they always managed a small income, enough for flour, tea, sugar, tobacco and petrol to go out and catch a kangaroo or a rabbit.

"Yeah," said Blue, "I don't reckon we'll get a price now."

"Tomorra is our day," said Jim "jus' 'magine, Blue, we'll be stung right up dis time tomorra."

"You know, Jim, I think I take it easy tomorra, I'm not feelin' too well, bin a bit crook. So, you see,

I'm not worried if I get a price now," said Old Bluey

"Jesus, Blue, don't die on me before pension day; after pension it's orright. I'll be able to take a charge up with me to the cemitry and when dey bury you, I'll cry my eyes out," said Jim, making a joke of it.

"Don't talk rot," said Blue, "You know I don't like um talk about funerals and cemitries."

"Yeah, sorry mate, I didn't think," said Jim, patting Blue on the back.

You see, it was a sad day when old Blue's missus died of cancer at the age of thirty five. That was twenty years ago and old Blue still felt the effects, even more than leaving the reserve. He never got over it. He felt half of his spirit went with Topsy. He had young Louie, but he was in Perth drinking himself to death, around parks or in Nyoongars' houses, helping other Nyoongars to fight their fights amongst their own relations.

Young Louie was a good boy growing up until he went into the army. Then he went off to Vietnam, done a tour. When he came back, all he wanted to do was drink, drink and drink, all the time. Maybe it would have been better if he got shot over there, instead of drinking himself to death. I think that Vietnam made him go off his head, thought Blue.

"Well," said Blue, "It's getting dark now, Jim, old mate. I think I'll go and lay down an' be up bright an' early."

"Okay," said Jim, "I'll come around early

tomorra and we head off to the post office together. You feeling orright, Blue?"

"Yeah, not too bad," said Blue.

"See ya," said Jim, wandering off into the night.

Jim was up bright and early and made his way to Blue's place. Funny, thought Jim, a group of Nyoongars all crying around, maybe they brought some bad news to old Blue about young Louie, he's always in the shit. Jim quickened his stride but wasn't prepared for the shock, as he came within talking distance.

"He gone, old Uncle Bluey died in his sleep last night," cried a Nyoongar woman, sobbing from her heart and holding a babe in her arms.

"No, no," cried Jim, "not my old mate, my old cuzzin," as he ran for the back door. "He can't die on me, not today, it's pension day."

Eleven

The Wool Pickers

"Well," said Barney to his nephew, "It's a good day for wool pickin', unna."

"Yeah, Unc," said Bill, looking up at the early morning sun, "It's gunna get hot later on."

"What ya reckon, feel like comin' out?" asked Barney.

"'Course, you know me, Uncle, bugger all else to do, runnin' low on tucker, dole cheque next week, hell, dunno how we gunna live 'til then," responded Bill.

"Right," said the old fella, "I'll get the ute ready an' tell Auntie Florrie you an' me goin' out. You tell your yorgah too."

"'Course, Unc, gotta tell my yorgah, she growlin' cruel already . . . Get off your black hole, Bill an' do somethin' solid, not wanna muntj alla time," said Bill mimicking his woman.

The old uncle laughed as he watched his nephew walk away. When you an' your yorgah fight, even the good Lord ducks for cover, he thought, laughing to himself while making off to tell his wife, Florrie, he was going wool picking.

Barney and Florrie were in their late sixties and, for fifty of those years, they had been together through thick and thin, through the days of alcoholic stupor and nights of alcoholic amnesia — and they were still together. Their three children, two boys and a girl, were living in Perth. All had good jobs and, most importantly, they had lives of their own.

Barney often cursed himself for not having a clear head when they were growing up. Thankfully, they'd understood the lack of opportunities there'd been for the Nyoongar community in a small wheatbelt town.

"Me an' Bill goin' out to see if we can get some wool," said Barney to his wife Florrie.

"You might gotta go long way out. Nyoongars bin pickin' close here," she said.

"Boyyah, any?" he asked and in the same breath added, "You know, petrol," knowing his wife usually had some put away somewhere. Ever since they both gave up the grog about fifteen years ago, she always had enough till next pension day.

"Ready, Unc?" asked Bill carrying his waterbag, seeing Aunty Florrie he added, "How you bin, Aunty Florrie?"

"I bin good since I chuck away that stinkin' gerbah," she replied, shaking her head.

"Yeah, you two look solid now," said Bill. Since these two gave up the gerbah, they seemed so full of life. They looked better than the younger one's still on the gerbah, he thought.

"Boyyah wa, or you gimme, unna?" Barney asked, searching his pockets.

"Take 'em, here," Florrie said, passing a ten dollar note to Barney.

"How many bags you got, Unc?" asked Bill.

"'bout five empty wheat bags," replied Barney.

"Let's bulyaka then," suggested Bill.

"You gottem gun?" asked Florrie.

"Yeah, under seat. You make 'em big damper. Might get yonga," he said, as he and Bill prepared to leave.

He started the ute and pulled away from the house, both of them waving to Florrie. As they headed north, they could see that the hot summer sun had already done its damage to the landscape. Only five months ago, this land was covered by lush green crops of wheat and a thick carpet of glistening green grass. Seeing it now, with it's lack of rain, even had the sand restless with a strong breeze. But the breezes in the summer, were so far and few between that the soil, with its great patience, suffered the onslaught of the menacing sun.

Nothing was said between the uncle and nephew. Barney moved along at a steady pace. He didn't want to go too fast in this heat. He was afraid the radiator might boil.

Gotta get it fixed next pension day, he thought. Come next pension, it'll still be the same. When he was travelling within his own Shire boundary he never had to worry, but with trips like this, it always came to his attention. He cursed himself out aloud.

"Hey, wassa matter, Unc?" asked Bill, wondering if his old uncle had lost his marbles.

"Nothing . . . um orright, jus' dis bloody radiator. Keep meanin' to get him fixed. I don't worry about him till I go on trips like dis," he growled

"How far you reckon we come, Unc?" asked Bill, keeping his eye on the temperature gauge.

"Might be twenty miles, might be more," he replied.

"Let's try the first farm we come to, Unc," said Bill, not wanting to be stuck in the middle of nowhere on this hot day.

Barney slowed the ute down and turned left towards the farm house. He could see that the sheep were very thin as they ran away from the oncoming vehicle. Rain and feed are very scarce out this way, too, thought Barney.

"Reckon he got some dead ones here," said Bill, noticing the condition of the sheep.

"By, gee, that cold weather we had in the winter musta downed a few," replied Barney.

"Wonder if any Nyoongars been this way?" asked Bill. Slowing the ute down in front of the house, they were greeted by barking dogs that seemed to come from nowhere.

"Where in the hell these poxy dawgs come from?" called out Barney, winding his window up. There were about five sheep dogs running around his ute, barking and pissing all over the tyres. One big bastard was standing on his hind legs with his front paws leaning against Barney's door, barking furiously at him.

"Bugger dis!" said Barney, counting the fangs on the mutt's jaw.

"Shoo! G'orn! Get!" shouted Bill, also winding his window up very quickly.

Barney looked at his nephew and with a smile on his face, said, "G'orn, go up to the house an' knock on the front door."

"You gotta be jokin', Uncle, I'd rather fight ten drunken Nyoongars than wrestle with these poxy dawgs."

"Ni, boss comin' now," said Barney, pointing towards the house.

"Dus him, orright," called Bill, watching him come towards the ute.

"Go on, piss off, you bastard," shouted the boss, as the slinking dogs moved on his command.

Winding the window down, Barney said, "Thanks, boss, I was a bit frighten' for awhile."

"Don't have to worry about them," said the boss, "More than likely to lick you to death."

Dus what you reckon, thought Barney. That big bastard lookin' me in the eye would frighten the shit out of the devil himself, he got more teeth than a crocodile, an' more sharper.

"Well, what can I do for you?" asked the boss.

Good, thought Barney, no Nyoongars been out here. Getting out of the ute and looking to see if the coast was clear, he asked, "Wondering if you got any dead wool around the place?"

"Dead wool?" asked the boss, confused.

"You know," said Barney, "Any sheep died over the winter months."

"Oh, I understand now," said the boss, registering to this old Aboriginal man, "As a matter of fact, I have. That cold snap we had at the end of May and the beginning of June, that really took its toll on the sheep. Out in the west paddock, there were quite a few that didn't survive."

"Be orright if we have a look?" asked Barney.

"I suppose it's okay. As long as you shut the gates behind you and try not to frighten the sheep. I hate to see my sheep running around on a day like this," he said.

"Dus true, Boss," said Barney, "we be careful orright."

"Also beware of your exhaust pipe when you travel over the stubble." The boss and Barney checked under the ute.

"Your exhaust looks safe. Okay, then . . . and don't forget the gates," said the boss.

"We won't," said Barney.

"Oh, by the way," said the boss, "I guess you blokes wouldn't have won that four million dollars in last night's Lotto draw?" walking away laughing.

What dat yortj talkin' 'bout, thought Barney, four million dollars and I won't be here pickin' your dead wool, shaking his head and getting into the ute.

"Choo, you solid, Unc," said Bill, with dollar signs in his eyes.

"Yeah," said Barney, "As soon as he said, 'What can I do for you?' I knew Nyoongars never been here."

They had to go through three gates before hitting their jackpot. Barney drove carefully through the paddocks, keeping away from the high stubble. Barney himself climbed out with Bill to shut the gates.

"Here, look, Unc," shouted Bill, pointing.

There, before their very eyes, dead sheep lay everywhere. The winter had been cruel to these sheep that had yet to be shorn. Barney and Bill quickly and happily ripped the wool from the dead carcasses. These dead sheep had been lying here for six months or more, perished in the winter and dried by the summer. The stench and the blowflies didn't deter the eager hands that shook the fleece from the bones, brushing the blowflies away and exposing the maggots that cringed in fear under the deadly heat of the sun. The crows cawed out joyfully for the rotting flesh that would be their feast when left behind by eager hands. The dead wool, sold in all its stinking glory, would put food on the table, petrol in the tank and smoke back into the lungs of the two men.

"Das all, Unc," cried Bill, sweating profusely as he hoisted the last of the five fully-packed bags into the back of the ute.

"Gawd, dis place stink," called out Barney, not realizing he'd been in the middle of the stench for the last two hours.

"Let's bulyaka then, Unc," said Bill, with a satisfied smile on his face.

"Yeah, you have boyyah till your pay now," smiled Barney edging his way through the gates and past the farmhouse. He wanted to thank the farmer for giving him permission to pick his dead wool, but there was no life around except the dogs and he wanted to get away from them as quickly as possible.

The drive back was more in a satisfied manner than the eagerness of the drive coming out, for he and Bill had done quite a job back there.

"How much we get for this lot?" asked Bill.

"Orrr, dunno. Might be hundred dollars, might be more," said the old fella with a twinge of tiredness in his voice.

"Never mind, Unc, long as my yorgah get some money, she'll be happy," said Bill happily.

"The first thing um gunna do is have a shower an' tell Florrie to get some mutton flaps," he said feeling the hunger pangs starting to attack his stomach and also realizing that the stench was quite powerful in the cab of the ute.

"I hope Aunty Florrie made that big damper. I wanna get some off youse,"said Bill feeling the same.

"Nearly home soon," said Barney, not worrying about the radiator as he put his foot down on the pedal.

"Hey, Unc, what that watjella said back at his farm? Something 'bout four million dollars, I thought he said four million sheep was dead. I was happy cruel, look," laughed Bill.

"Naw," Barney said, laughing, "Four million lotto draw last night."

"What if you had four million dollars, Unc, what you do?" asked Bill.

"Well . . . " laughed Barney, "first thing I do is give my kids a million each."

"What you an' Aunty Florrie gunna do with your million?" asked Bill, laughing.

"Um gunna take Auntie Florrie to dat French River place, somewhere. And next we be goin' to see that Nyoongar bloke. You know, he was locked up in jail for twenty years. An' come out to run his own country, wass his name?" asked Barney.

"Orr, yeah, Unc, I know. Orr . . . Nelson Mandela, yeah, Unc, das him. Anyway, Unc, what you wanna meet him for?" wondered Bill.

"Look, young Bill, all I wanna do is shake his han' an' tell him he horse of a Nyoongar orright. After bein' locked up alla time. Come out an' be boss of his own country. He moorditj orright."

"But he not Nyoongar, Unc. He South African," Bill explained to his old Uncle.

"He still moorditj, anyway," said Barney driving through town and slowly making his way to the Woolbuyers.

As he pulled up outside Willie, the Woolbuyer's shed, Bill said to his old uncle,

"Never mind, Unc, you sit here an' rest. I'll

take 'em into Willie's." Barney watched his young nephew unload and take the bags into the woolshed. It wasn't all that long before Bill came out with a smile on his face and, passing the cheque to Barney, said, "We got one hundred dollars for that lot, one dollar a kilo, he give. Das orright, unna?"

Barney was pleased as he headed for the bank to cash it. He gave forty dollars to Bill, whilst he kept sixty to cover fuel for the car. He dropped off Bill, who lived close by and headed home for a shower.

"You get 'em newspaper?" asked Florrie as Barney stepped inside.

"What you wanna paper for?" he asked, "Anyway um gonna have a shower. Here, boyyah, cause you goin' down town an' get me some flaps," he said, passing the money to her.

After he'd showered and got himself cleaned up, he sat and had a cup of tea; it was peaceful and quiet. He kept wondering why Florrie wanted that paper. Barney couldn't read or write so he often got Florrie to read for him. He knew she was a good reader, even at the ripe age of seventy. Moorditj yorgah, he thought.

Florrie came in carrying the shopping bags and put them on the table. "Gawd, still warm outside," she said.

"You get 'em paper?" he grunted.

"Course," she said, grabbing the newspaper and taking off into the bedroom. He watched her pick up her reading glasses and saw her back disappear. Within minutes, the warm peaceful humidity of the early evening was shattered by a piercing scream.

"Choo, aye, wassa matta?" shouted Barney, jolted back to reality and running into the bedroom. He froze in his tracks.

His wife was sprawled on her back across the bed, white as a ghost, shouting, "Gawd, gawd, thank you, Granny Maud."

Barney was speechless. Granny Maud had died forty years ago when he and Florrie first got together as pups. Granny Maud had always called them pups and she was eighty when she died, their first child was two then.

"I think I win plenty of boyyah!" was Florrie's only response when she came to. She composed herself and told him about the other day. She was lying on the bed, having a cry and thinking of Barney, old as he was, always going out to pick dead wool to put food on the table till next pension day. Then she looked up and saw the spirit of Granny Maud, clapping her hands and smiling at her, then she disappeared. After that, when she walked down town, she saw on a poster at the newsagents in big bold letters "FOUR MILLION DOLLARS to be won tonight" and she went in and bought a ticket. She had just checked her numbers with the paper, and she had gotten six numbers correct.

Still trembling, he asked, "What Granny Maud got to do with it?"

Florrie told him when she had the last two

children, her spirit was by the bed, smiling and clapping as she was giving birth.

"Look at our beautiful children now. Granny Maud only brought good luck to me," she whispered. She was thinking of Barney and the kids, especially Barney, wanting to take 'im to see that black man who was put in jail an' came out to be boss of his own country, before they both passed away.

Barney grabbed and hugged her. With tears in his eyes, he whispered in her ear, "He not Nyoongar, he South African."

Twelve

Uncle Dollar

"Gimme dollar?" asked Uncle Dollar to no one in particular. Ted, Mum and myself were standing around a warm, open fire in our backyard.

"What you wanna a dollar for, Bill?" asked Mum, Uncle Dollar's sister, rubbing her hands on this bitterly cold morning.

Bill was Uncle Dollar's real name. The Nyoongar community gave him the name 'Dollar' because everytime he saw a Nyoongar on the street, or wherever, he'd ask for a dollar. If they had, they would give. Eventually he'd end up with a price for a bottle of plonk.

"Look, Bill, you same as me, you got your pension yesterday, what? You been boozin' it already? Choo, shame, shoutin' all those young yorgahs. No shame, ol' man like you, my old brother, justa 'bout seventy, still jerripin for young yorgahs. Go away, you silly old rooster," Mum said, shaking her head as she walked back into the house.

That really got Ted and me laughing. When Mum opened up on her older brother, she let him have it with both barrels and at point blank range.

"What you young fuckers laughin' 'bout?" scowled Uncle Dollar.

"We're not laughing at you, Uncle Dollar," stammered Ted, "we're laughing at Mum, unna, Ross?" looking for my assistance.

"Course, Uncle, look," I said, trying to stop myself from laughing and making the sign of the cross at the same time.

"Well, gimme dollar, den, all um tryin' tuh do is getta price," he said looking at us with those old, sad, grey eyes, his hands outstretched towards us, his whole body trembling as he wiped a tear from his eye.

When Uncle Dollar developed that pose, it was hard for anyone to ignore him; even the meanest of the mean would succumb to him.

"Here, Uncle," I said, swallowing a lump in my throat, "seven dollars here."

"I think you'd better change your name to Ten Dollar Bill, 'cause that's all I got," said Ted, passing over the note.

"Thank you, uncles," he said with glee, "I think I stick to one dollar. If I go any higher, Nyoongars won't talk to me, think 'um gettin' too big for my boots," he chuckled, "an' don't tell dat ol' gal," he said sternly.

"We won't tell her," I said.

"What time, boy?" he inquired.

"Half past eight," replied Ted.

"Good, liquor store will be open now, I'll go an' getta leg opener for Lucie," he laughed, making off into the cold morning.

"Choo, Unc, you old buntji man," shouted Ted. Then turning to me, he said, "When I'm about seventy-odd I hope I can still get a horn."

"Yeah," I said, "If the heart can stand it, I'm sure the old yortj will stand up."

Uncle Dollar bought his bottle of plonk and headed for the public toilet for a mouthful. Lifting the bottle to his lips, he felt the dark, red liquid tear at his throat before hitting the bottom of his stomach, exploding inside of him and nearly ripping his toenails off their hinges.

Gawd! he thought, If dis don't open Lucie's legs up, I'll rape King Kong. He chuckled to himself, 'magine me tryin' to do dat to 'im? He took another swig and felt the warmth spread through his body, then wrapping his coat around his frail person, he stepped out of the toilet and walked onto the street. He noticed a few Nyoongars around and stopped for a yarn with them. They greeted him with, "Hello, Dollar," . . . "Choo, gettin' cold, unna, Dollar?" . . . "Winter 'ere, Dollar?"

His reply was always, "Gimme dollar, yeah winter 'ere."

He picked up about four extra dollars and headed for Lucie's house. Arriving at the gate, he was met by her big kangaroo dog, barking furiously at him

"Every fuckin' time I come here dis big poxy dawg wanna bite me. I'd love to get some turps and rub it on 'is ring," he grinned down at the dog.

Lucie came to the door, looking dishevelled and hungover as she shouted at Dollar, "What you doin' to my Tiger Boy?"

"Um doin' nothin' yet, but if you don't tie him up, um gunna piss all over 'im," came his reply.

"G'orn, you try, he'll bite your yortj off, not dat is any use to you," she sniggered, taking the dog around the back to tie him up.

Lucie was a woman in her middle-sixties. She liked old Uncle Dollar's company now that both their spouses were dead and their children were all grown up and living in the city. Uncle Dollar was about seven stone with his overcoat wringing wet, whereas Lucie was about sixteen stone with just a smile on her face. Behind her back, the Nyoongars called her, One Hundred Dollar Bill.

She called Dollar in and asked, "Got a charge?"

"Course, woman, I got im 'ere, slapping the right side of his coat."

Sitting at the kitchen table, glasses full, Lucie told him about last night's episode.

"Yeah, had a carton here last night and a flagon," she said taking a swig.

"Save any," he asked.

"Naw, too many here drinkin', an' when carton and flagon was finished, dey all fucked off. Meant to hide some for morning, got too drunk. I went lookin' for you."

"Choo, at Mona's?" he asked.

"Where else um gunna go lookin' for you? Anyway she said you was 'sleep, so I left you smellin' your hole. I came back and got drunk."

"I be fucked, neber mind," he said.

They yarned on, talking about nothing in particular, but mainly her kids and his kids, and how she was goin' to make a big damper and cook a pan full of kangaroo meat for Dollar, sayin' he was so thin . . . to which he immediately responded in a dignified manner.

"Hey, big girl, Um built like your Tiger Boy outside, all ribs and yortj."

"I can see your ribs stickin' out, but I don't know about your yortj," she said, laughing.

"When dat sticks out, you gunna be first to know," he said hopefully.

"Yeah, dus when dey bring back da pounds, shillings and pence," she said laughing.

That got Uncle Dollar into fits of laughter.

"Neber mind, Dollar, you're moorditj company orright," she said, "Anyway, is Mona's two boys still dere or dey gone back to Perth?"

"Naw, those two young fuckers still der, might be goin' back tomorra or next day. Dey gimme price for a bottle, dey good boys," he said, rubbing the stubble on his face.

"Nearly finished now, Dollar, gimme dat price?" she asked.

"Hang on, puddin' pie," he said, slurring his voice.

"What! You must be fuckin' drunk, you talkin' like dat, what next? You be lookin' for sleep, you big kangaroo dawg," she said laughing.

"Not dis ol' black magic," he slurred, as he put six one dollar coins on the table.

"No wonder dey call you Dollar Bill," she said grabbing the coins, "You have the last bit, l go down and get a charge."

"G'orn den," he said drowsily.

"Don't you fuckin' go to sleep on me," she scowled.

"I'll piss myself for a week if you got on toppa me," he laughed drunkenly.

"You know what um talkin' 'bout, you silly ol' doodle. With my sixteen stone, I'll crush you to death," she said, going to get ready.

Yeah, he thought to himself, if I got on toppa Lucie, I'll be like an ant on top of Uluru.

"Goin' now," she called, as she headed to the door.

This left Uncle Dollar finishing the last drop of port. He decided to lay down and have a rest until she came back.

"Goin' now," shouted Ted, as I packed my bags and headed to the car.

"Can't you boys stay a little bit longer," pleaded Mum to us both.

Guiltily, Ted and I looked at each other, then responded quickly, "Work, Mum."

I walked back to her and hugged her, whispering, "You know Ted and I love you."

"Yeah," said Ted, "We would love to stay with you forever, but we must go back to work."

"Who is going to send you money if we don't go to work?" I said, softening her up.

"Course, den, I know you boys not like those other Nyoongars here. Got all their mob stuck in one house," she said rather crossly, wiping a tear from her eye, "You boys go to Lucie's and see dat silly ol' uncle of yours."

"Of course we will and you know we will," I said.

Ted and I were both torn between the love of our mother and society itself.

"Yeah, come on, Ross," said Ted getting in the car. We farewelled Mum and headed around to Lucie's place.

"Front door open," I said, as we got out of the car.

"Only her roo dog barking at the back," said Ted, hesitantly. We'd heard a lot of yarns about her dog, not only from Uncle Dollar, but also from other Nyoongars, who reckon her Tiger Boy had bitten Nyoongars who'd come around looking for a drink. The dog was always chastised but never beaten.

As Uncle Dollar would always say, "A good kangaroo dawg will always look after himself and the Nyoongar community, not like these 'holier-than-thou' Nyoongars with their prissy dogs," but not in those exact words.

"Ni, they must be muntjin," whispered Ted, listening for creaking bed springs.

"Go away," I laughed, "I know they both cart-warras, but they wouldn't leave the front door open."

"Uncle Dollar," shouted Ted, as we went inside.

"Here," I said pointing.

"Hey, Uncle! Wake up, we got a young yorgah here, stripped naked, ready to rape you," laughed Ted.

"Choo, your fly is open and your yortj is hanging out," I laughed.

"G'orn, you two young fuckers, you tease your uncle, you'll both end up with bald heads," shouted Uncle Dollar.

We all went into the kitchen and had a good old yarn with Uncle Dollar, who always had us laughing with his bizarre and humorous stories. We could see he was getting very impatient with Lucie's absence.

He started muttering "Gawd, I wish this big tuppy hurry up, man wanna drink."

"Choo, Unc, you shouldn't talk about your big yorgah like that," said Ted, laughing.

"Any bigga, she be wearin' a chaff bag for a dress," he laughed.

"I'll tell her what you said, Unc," I laughed.

"Aye, look out, no, don't. She make me piss if I said dat to her face," he said, looking at the door.

"Never mind, Unc, we'll let you live a little bit longer."

"We won't tell her," said Ted, getting up from the table.

"What, you fullas goin' now?" asked Uncle

Dollar.

"Yep, unna, Ross, we gotta go," replied Ted, looking for my assistance.

"Yeah, Unc, at the end of this highway there's a precious bit of sunshine waiting for me in that grey city," I said, remembering those words I found in a grade two schoolbook somewhere.

"What you talkin' 'bout, you think you watjella, or what?" came Uncle Dollar's somewhat confused reply.

"Let's bulyaka then," said Ted, making for the door.

"Here, Unc, fifteen dollars for your next leg opener," I said, hugging him and laughing.

"Tell dat big, beautiful, 'skinny' yorgah to come along if you see her," he shouted, laughing to himself.

"Yeah, Unc," I responded.

Ted drove through the town slowly as I scanned the streets for Lucie. There were quite a few Nyoongars in town, all our relations, grannies, uncles, aunties, and cousins. All waved out to us, the dignified, the conservative, the drunk, the sober, the lame, the blind, the Christians and the non-Christians. All Nyoongars and I was proud to be one of them . . . but no Lucie.

"You see Lucie?" Ted asked.

"Naw," I said, waving and looking through smiling faces. "You wouldn't believe it, here is a woman, bigger than the Statue of Liberty, yet we can't see her in a little country town."

"Only you can say something like that, Rossie Boy, no one else," Ted said, laughing.

"Let's head for the city," I said, feeling quite low.

"Never mind, koordah, we'll be back soon to see Mum, Uncle Dollar and our mob," said Ted in a sombre manner.

"Yeah," I said, watching the sheep and cattle safely tucked away in their paddocks nibbling at the green shoots that had followed the rain. As the kilometres disappeared under our wheels, the trees were disappearing very quickly, and I closed my eyes to pray to Mother Earth to look after Mum, Uncle Dollar and all our mob, before dropping off to a restless sleep.

The motor played a beautiful tune in the back of my mind and as my dreams started to unfold I found they were about Mum and Dad (rest his soul), sitting around the campfire with Uncle Dollar telling them about his magical Dreamtime stories.

"Hey, wake up, Rossie," I heard a voice coming from as far back as the Dreamtime calling me by my Aboriginal name, not my European name, but the name Uncle Dollar used on me when I was a child. A beautiful name associated with the trees, rocks, sun, and the sand. Only once he called me that name, never since. Just before disappearing from my dream, he kept saying, "I be gone soon, Rossie."

"We'll be home soon," called Ted, jolting me back to reality.

"Ugh, wow," I said, yawning, "Had a wicked dream about Uncle Dollar, wonder if he's alright?" I asked, stretching.

"Funny you should say that," said Ted, in a way that only Nyoongars understand. He explained that not far from Perth, where a lot of Nyoongars live, he thought he saw Uncle Dollar as he drove through, not far from a group, with his head bowed, and he really felt sad for him.

"No, he's two hundred k's away. Impossible, he doesn't own a private jet," he said laughing, weaving his way through the thick city traffic.

"Let's ring Mum," I said, laughing at the last remark.

Arriving at our flat, we rushed inside and Ted, being the eldest, rang Mum. She told us that Uncle Dollar had collapsed and died inside Lucie's house. He had had a major heart attack.

"He finished now," she said, wailing. Then she asked how we knew, and we told her about my dream and Ted seeing him in a town standing on his own away from a group of Nyoongars.

"You two only ones who cared for him," she sobbed, "not even his own boy. That was his way of tellin' he goin'."

Through our own sorrow and the sorrows of the families concerned, we managed to organize the funeral. On the funeral day, Nyoongars came from everywhere by the busloads - north, south, east, west and Alice Springs. Just before they lowered the coffin down, Ted and I put a dollar coin each on the coffin. Mum sobbed and turned to us and whispered, “He only want one.”

Slowly, as we escorted Mum out towards the cemetery gates, we felt his presence with us.

“I told you he only wanted one, look down at your shoes, Rossie,” sobbed Mum in barely a whisper.

Looking down at my shoes, I saw among the loose sand, a dollar coin. Even in death . . . all he wanted was a dollar . . .

Thirteen

The Last Drop

"Yeah, I bin 'member, when I was youn' fella, lotta trees an' birds, bin 'ere plenty. Talk 'bout too much, look now, you bin see um nothink," said seventy five year old Tommy Toothpick to his old seventy two year old watjella mate.

"Yeah," responded Old Billy Jangels, taking a swig from the cheap bottle of plonk they had just bought from the liquor store. It was a beautiful warm spring day at Heirisson Island and Yagan's statue looked out across the Swan River with forlorn hope. "'magine ol' Yagan, bin swimmin', kill um yonga, kill um watjella mans an' robbin' um an' turn 'round an' muntj dere watjella womans. He bin only now stan'in' 'round for birds to piss on 'im," chuckled Old Tommy.

Old Billy, with a wry smile on his face, responded, “At least they got a statue of Yagan. What have you got”?

“Well . . . , ” my said sardonically,“ I bin got my ol’ yortj. Eben when I gettum yorgah ’im neber stan’ up like Yagan, ’im lay down low eben when da yorgahs show me dere tuppies.” Old Tommy’s laughing got Old Billy into fits of laughter.

Old Tommy and Billy, both heavy drinkers and from different backgrounds, had been drinking together for about five years or more. On and off, one or the other would end up in hospital over the freezing winter months, sometimes both. The welfare groups, who brought around soup and sandwiches to the homeless people of Perth, tried to encourage the two elderly gentlemen to go to an old men’s home, hostel or even a refuge for men. But they had a better chance to get the devil, himself, to go to a confession on a Sunday morning at the Catholic Church and receive the Holy Communion, than to get those two old boys into an old men’s home. They both agreed it was only for walking sticks or wheel chair jobs.

Regardless of age, they were quite able to roam the parks of Perth looking for a charge or gnumeeries. On their journey through the streets, they would pick up bumpers (cigarette ends) and with their cigarette papers, they would roll the bumpers up right on the street, on St. George’s Terrace in Perth, much to the disgust of the high-flying executives or entrepreneurs, who walked with their mobile phones glued to their ears. These high-fliers would look at the two old blokes, one real dark and the other white, with utter contempt and disgust as they hurried to their offices overlooking the Swan River. It never fazed Old Tommy or Old Billy.

After walking around the parks, they'd always run into someone, who either had a flagon of plonk or a cask of moselle, or some sort of alcoholic liquid. When they'd get too drunk, they'd sleep in whatever park they got pissed in. There was no animosity between the odd couple, even when pissed out of their heads. There was rarely a heated argument between the two, which was quite incredible for two old piss heads. Old Tommy would actually come to the defence of Old Billy, when he was on the receiving end of some drunken Nyoongars. But the troublemakers were mainly strange Nyoongars who didn't know him. As Old Tommy would say, "Blow-in blackfellas from da country. Keep 'way from dem." The worst part came when they were getting over the grog. Going through the withdrawal symptoms, the D.T.'s or the rats, was a nightmare for them. They'd see snakes crawling towards them, pink elephants running around the park, or even a crocodile about to attack them . . . in the parks of Perth. One night, Old Tommy even talked to Elvis Presley and this was in 1988.

The yarns they'd tell . . . like the day Captain Cook got lost in his ship and landed in this country. He was that pissed from all the rum he'd been drinking, that on seeing land, he told his convicts to put a dinghy down. He staggered into the boat with some flag and when he touched land, he put this flag out to steady himself and the fuckin' thing stuck in the ground, thereby claiming this country while asleep under the flag. While all the convicts got stuck into the rum laughing at this, Captain Cook lay under the flag pissed out of his head. Old Tommy would often say, when pissed, "It's dem jail birds from Englun' who claimed dis country, not da fuck'n drunken' Cook."

Old Billy would agree but, in his mind disagree because of his white upbringing. The more he listened to Old Tommy on the foundation of this land, the more he saw and listened. Ostracism was quite evident amongst Tommy and his people and the more he socialised with Tommy and his lot, he himself found what 'ostracised' really meant. His own people classed him as an unworthy refugee. Not that Old Billy cared, for he found the real people in Old Tommy and his drinking mates. They were the ones who cared and looked after him, always finding space in the park for him to sleep. Not that there wasn't much space around the park. But it was good to wake up in the park and Old Tommy would be there with a charge, saying "'Ere, my brother, you bin hab dis charge," as he passed over a bottle of plonk that kept the crocodile from attacking.

There was a lot of humour among the Nyoongars he was drinking with. Yarns or make up yarns were forever flowing. Laughter was a constant reminder of the freedom of the parks. There were no wars, no drug overdoses and suicide wasn't even a thought. No mortgage to pay, no rent. Not even society's domineering attitude towards the people of the park would change their existence. There was the occasional fight through jealousy between man and woman or two blokes got stuck into each other over a yorgah. This wasn't a regular event but when it did happen, it was more of a comedy spectacle than a world championship fight of the century.

No one quite knew where Old Tommy had come from and Old Tommy himself wasn't too sure. Some say the Kimberley, Alice Springs, Hermannsburg, Namitjira's country or down south in Western Australia, or at Kalgoorlie in the Goldfields. He'd often classified himself as a Wongi, which no Nyoongar questioned because of his Goldfields Aboriginal features. Then again, he'd tell them of his Yamitji upbringing, an Aboriginal from Carnarvon. No one questioned him. It was taken for granted that he did come from that way. He also spoke of his upbringing in Leigh Creek on the Flinders Rangers in South Australia, that he was a member of the Adnyamathanha people and he spoke the Yura Ngawarla language fluently as well as Wongi, Yamitji and some of the Northern Territory tongues, mainly around Alice Springs. As Old Billy would say to their drinking mates, "Old Tommy here, is a fuckin' walkin' encyclopedia."

But what intrigued Old Tommy was the statue

of Yagan, standing so proud, strong and tall and holding that spear across the nape of his neck. He'd often think of Yagan with all the mob he'd be drinking with and say "You know when um bin dead, I won' um to buil' a big statue ob me, stan'in' with a flagon in my han' on top ob da Flinders Rangers," chuckling to himself.

"Yeah, you reckon you Wongi," one would say laughing, or

"I thought you Yamitji" or

"Na, you reckon you Nyoongar from da sou' west"

"But you reckon Namitjira your mob." All laughed, including Old Tommy himself.

Old Tommy could spin a yarn that would leave the mob around the parks with cramps for a week from laughing hoarsely. Indeed he was a man of talent in the comedy field. He always told them, "When I bin youn' boy, I tell um my father I wanna be when I grow 'em up. I be clown," he said laughing.

"An' what your father say?" said a voice amongst all the laughter.

Laughing with the mob and trying to regain himself between the mirth, he responded. "'im say you be clown from da day you bin born an' you bin die clown."

This got the mob rockin' with laughter as the flagon of plonk passed around the circle. During the laughter, it was quite impossible to have a guzzle of plonk normally. The laughter would mingle with the sound of the wind, the trucks, buses and cars and the birds in the trees and children squealing with delight as they played in the vastness of the park. Old Tommy and Billy and all the mob would experience happiness at its best. The happiness they indulged in was for this particular day. Yesterday didn't exist, tomorrow will come to them, they didn't belong to tomorrow. As far as they were concerned this hour and time could last forever. The yarns would go on and on, along with the laughter. Until some one, pissed out of his brain, would drop off to sleep in the warm sun with the rest keeping sentry over him.

Old Tommy and his old mate Billy (but mainly Old Tommy) would go down to the railway station and would cadge the commuters there. They always ended up with a price for a flagon or a cask, whichever they felt like drinking on that particular day. They'd always end up with their gnumeeries and off they'd go to some park in Perth to have a charge and a yarn with some Nyoongars.

If Old Tommy didn't feel like drinking with the mob, he'd say to Old Billy, "Come on den, we go to Yagan's." To Old Billy that meant in the bushes around Yagan's statue.

In his own mind, Tommy, to a certain degree, was affiliated with Yagan. He'd often let his thoughts drift back to the days of Yagan. When Old Billy was asleep in the warm sun, half shot out of his head or just plain pissed, Old Tommy would sip on his plonk and imagine himself as one of Yagan's warriors, fighting the watjellas away from the beauty and grandeur of the Swan River. Little did Yagan know, he thought, how these fuckin' watjellas can fuck beauty up so much. I wish dey all fuck off back to Englun', Old Tommy thought, feeling the anger rise within himself. Looking at the cars speeding along the causeway and the Esplanade, he imagined the Swan River long before the convicts had arrived here and the bush was thick and untouched. The water flowing freely towards the sea, feeling the marine life swimming and playing deep inside it's belly and the warm sun reflecting upon her. This was Yagan's paradise. Food that belongs to the bushes that surrounded the river was in abundance and the food which lived in the belly of the river was caught by the Nyoongars, bare hands, not to profit by the food in her belly, but to keep the tribes adequately supplied. Even the kangaroos that lived off the lush green grass on the banks were plentiful. The Nyoongars stalked their prey in the thick foliage, taking out the male kangaroo with a spear and letting the female kangaroo hop off into the bush to tend to her little one.

"G'orn den, Toothpick, tell us another yarn," quipped one of his drinking mates amongst all the jabbering and laughing mob in the park.

"Tell us about the time you was talking to Elvis," encouraged Old Bill.

"What dat singer, da king," replied one Nyoongar with a smirk on his face.

"Why, he been dead for ten years or more," stated another.

The next minute all the Nyoongars started to sing Elvis Presley songs, from his first hit single to his last. One yorgah got up and started dancing and singing *Jailhouse Rock*. Another got up and doing likewise to *Wooden Heart*. One yorgah, dancing with her man, started to punch into him because of the words he sang, "We can't go on together . . . " This left the Nyoongar man lying flat on his back, seeing stars and his yorgah standing over him in a drunken stupor saying, "You, you big black prunes. I don't care who you hab. I can getta big black yortj, anytime I want."

"Hey, Tommy, you'd better tell that yarn about Elvis or you'll have the mob singin', dancin' and fightin'," said Old Bill pleading.

Looking at his audience with amazement and disbelief, Old Tommy thought to himself, to dees mob, dat Presley not dead yet. Looking at one yorgah trying to dance like Elvis and sing, only to fall down legs up in the air, "Cunt up she bin fall," laughing at her and nudging Old Bill, who was also laughing, not only at that yorgah who fell over, but the others trying to sing and dance like Elvis.

"C'mon, Tommy, if you don't settle these mob down you gonna have the riot squad here," pleaded Bill.

"Dey bin fuckin shoot us all den," responded Old Tommy. He knew how to get their attention by grabbing the flagon and having a charge, then he yelled out, "Hey, you mob wanna charge or what?" He heard words of "Course," "Fuckin' oath" and

"Git dis woman offa me. She tryin' to dance and muntj me at da same time."

Roars of laughter erupted from the Nyoongars as they staggered into an orderly manner to sit in a circle. All eyeing the flagon in Tommy's hand.

"Gimme charge," said one Nyoongar.

"I tell you what, Elbis got fuck-all on you lot," laughed Old Tommy, passing the flagon around.

"Tell 'em that yarn," said Old Billy, grabbing the flagon.

"Dus true" said Tommy. Then whispering to Old Billy, "Betta not talk 'bout him, Mummid Ali, cause dey be gittin up fightin'," laughed Old Tommy.

"No, no, don't," laughed Old Billy. "G'orn den, tell us what Elbis said to you," urged one yorgah.

"Okay," said Old Tommy thinking back on that night of 26 January 1988.

*

It was a warm night and he was sicker than a dog shitting razor blades. He had just jumped off the train at Guildford and walking around, saw that the pubs were all open. So he asked quite a few watjellas for a price for a bottle of plonk, seeing that they were celebrating the landing of the first convicts. He thought they might give him a price for a bottle, "but dey gib me fuck-all," he said. "Dey was more happy wid dem jail birds an' doin' da jail house rock den me."

After receiving knock back upon knock back,

he was disgruntled and afraid of going into the rats, so he decided to go across the railway line to the park there. Seeing that no one was around, he saw a big church and walked towards it. Sitting on the grass, he leaned his back to the wall and thought, Um fucked now, can't get um price for gerbah. Might be hab um sleep. Laying himself down against the wall and hoping he wouldn't go into alcoholic seizure just yet, he dozed off.

Suddenly, he jerked himself awake. "Hey, what dis," he said to himself, as he clenched and unclenched his fingers to stop them going into cramp. Again, he said to himself, "Mus' be sleepin' for 'while". Still laying on his right side, he saw the lights of a vehicle pull up. It was a big black car. Who dis, he thought, not munartj. Wondering, he saw the two back doors open and three men get out and make their way to Tommy Toothpick. The man in the middle was taller then the other two. Tommy looked again and thought, No . . . can't be! As they stood in front him, Old Tommy shot upright and said to the bloke in the middle. "I bin see you on T-bee. You bin dat singer, Sinatra somebody." The man he was referring to had thick black hair and long sideburns to his mouth. "No, dus right, you dat Elbis Presley," he nearly shouted. He saw a row of pearly white teeth and the man had dark glasses on.

In his southern American drawl, he said, "You look sick, man."

"L . . . l . . . look, Mr Presley, could you get me a drink," in his best mission vocabulary.

"Shouldn't there be a tap here?"

"No, no. Not that drink, you know, a flagon of wine and a packet of cigarettes, packet a Winfields red. Please, Mr Presley."

"I'll see what I can do, man," indicating to the other two fella's with him. They walked back to the big black car and got in.

"I mus' be dreamin'," he said to himself and even pinched himself. He walked around in circles. Wait 'til I tell dees other Nyoongars, he thought.

"But dey reckon he dead," he said to himself. "You goin' in da rats, Tommy Toothpick, Graylands for you." He saw the lights come back and Elvis and his two body guards came back towards him. One of the body guards passed him the flagon and the cigarettes.

Putting the flagon down at his feet and ripping the cover off his cigarettes, he asked, "I thought you dead."

"You see me now, don't ya, man," came the reply.

"Yeah, but Mr Pres . . . "

"Look, man, I got to go," shaking his hand.

"How you gittin' back?" asked Old Tommy.

"Lisa Marie," came the reply. And just before he walked away, he said to Old Tommy, "Pretend you didn't see me, man." He walked off and jumped in that big black car and took off.

*

"You lyin' old, black cunt," shouted one half pissed Nyoongar.

"No, no, dus true, look," making the sign of the cross on his chest.

"You talkin' outta your hole," called another.

"He bin dead for ten years or more," laughed one Nyoongar.

"Well, you gotta be da first blackfella to see him since he died," called another.

"Yeah," said Old Tommy.

*

Looking at Yagan's statue with forlorn hope. "No, dose blackfella's neber beliebed me when I tell um 'bout Elbis."

Old Billy laughed, full of mirth and passed the flagon over, saying, "I don't think a whitefella would believe you either."

"Yeah, dus true," said Old Tommy, watching a watjella man jogging towards the statue of Yagan. "Gawd, he look fuckin' drunk," as he started to wobble and fall right next to Yagan's statue.

"Hey, look at dis, a watjella man fall ober at Yagan's statue," trying to push Old Bill, who suddenly seemed to be asleep, with his feet. He watched other joggers run to the fallen man and a woman was shouting in her mobile phone. There were quite a few people around this prone figure.

"Here," he called to Old Bill, looking at the flagon, "Las' drop left."

Watching the activity around him, he saw an

ambulance arrive and put him on a stretcher, all covered with a sheet, and wheel him into the vehicle. He died he thought. “Well,” he said. “Yagan take um watjellas even when he dead.”

“Here, Bill, you old yortj. Las’ drop left,” trying to wake him and getting no response. He realized then that that was the last drink he had with Old Bill, next to Yagan’s statue. Getting up, he finished the last drop from the flagon. Looking down on his watjella mate, he said “Neber min’ ol’ cobber, I get yorgah to ring amb’lence up.” Walking away, he thought, ol’ Yagan take ’em two watjellas. One my mate, other I don’t know.

Fourteen

Charlie

Old Charlie, or should I say a young sixty year old Charlie, had just spent the night in jail and was let out in the morning. What was the offence? Drunk and disorderly, the coppers said. What a piddly charge, he thought, as he hobbled up Hannans Street, heading towards the park. He had spent his last five dollars bailing himself out.

The sergeant had made it quite clear before letting him out, "If you don't appear in court on Monday, you'll lose your five dollars. No one picks a fight with Paddy Hannan, not in Kalgoorlie."

Today's only Saturday, I've got all day to pull through. Gawd I've got to get myself on that train tonight for Perth somehow, he thought.

From what he could gather back at the police station, when the police had arrived after a complaint, Charlie couldn't get a drink out of his water-bag properly so he decided to punch and kick into poor old Paddy.

Paddy didn't feel a thing, he thought, as he looked down at his swollen right fist, and bent to lift his trouser leg up and inspect a swollen right foot. I was the silly bastard who copped the lot. Fancy me, a man with my intelligence, fighting a statue that's been sitting there for a hundred years or more.

The nephew who had brought him here had gone on to Meekatharra chasin' up some women. "Now I'm stuck in Kalgoorlie, not a cracker on me, dying for a bottle of port. Yeah, Charlie, old boy," he said to himself, "you have really hit rock bottom now. If only the Nyoongars you drink with in Perth could see you now. They'd piss themselves laughing."

The hide of that fresh-faced copper, just out of high school, suggesting they charge me with assault. How could you assault a statue? May as well lay in the park for a while 'til I can think straight, he thought.

He hobbled into the park and found a nice sunny spot to lay down and soak up the warm afternoon sun, listening to the children's laughter, the crows cawing in the trees and the breeze rustling among the leaves. My, what a beautiful blend of music, thought Charlie, Beats all the symphonies in the world. He dozed off.

When he came to, he heard horrible rock music that must have been coming from a transistor, because it stopped and the announcer came on. "Good afternoon to all you people out there listening to 6KG Kalgoorlie. The time is twenty past one on this warm sunny afternoon. I'll be playing some blasts from the past. As a matter of fact, I'm going to play one right now. It's called *My Boomerang Won't Come Back* by Charlie Drake. This was a number one hit in the mid-sixties."

Charlie had heard this song before, but most times he was half shot. This was the first time he ever heard it sober. The more he listened to the words of the song, the more evident it became that it was a watjella trying to throw that boomerang. How in the hell can a blackfella go black in the face trying to throw that thing? Maybe Captain Cook was a blackfella when he left England and when he saw the blackfellas here to welcome him, he turned white with fright. He lay back smiling to himself, enjoying the rest of the song.

Then he got an idea and with the last few remaining brain cells in his head, he tried to put it together. Just as Charlie Drake was about to finish his song, it came to him. He got up as quickly as he could. Gawd, this has to work, he thought, as he hobbled out of the park. If it works I'll have a skin full of booze, a ticket on the train and a bottle to take home.

He wandered the back alleys and lanes of Kalgoorlie, before coming on an old bloke and a young fella sitting under a peppercorn tree not far from the railway station. Charlie introduced himself to the old bloke and to the young fella. Then he sat down under the tree with them yarnin', not talking about anything in particular. Charlie found out that the young fella's name was Curtis and the old bloke, who looked to be in his mid-sixties, was called Uncle in English. He did have a Wongi name but Charlie couldn't pronounce it, so it was easier calling him Uncle than a name he couldn't get his tongue around.

Communicating with these two is hard, thought Charlie, especially since he was a Nyoongar himself. Gawd, a bloke needs an interpreter just to talk on basic subjects. But one subject he got through without any hassles was gerbah and by them doing the actions, he was a full bottle. And he was still crackin' for a bottle. The young fella asked how he hurt his hand. Charlie raised his eyes up to the heavens and asked forgiveness, then he told him how he had gotten into a big fight last night, knocking out four big policemen and it took ten of them to overpower him before locking him up. He sounded so convincing that he, himself, was starting to believe it. Then, realising young Curtis was looking at him as if he were Lionel Rose, decided to get off the subject. He thought this young fella would pick a fight with any living thing and expect him to back him up. Anyway, less they know about Paddy Hannan's statue the better.

So he laid his plan out on the red soil for them to see and explained very clearly and slowly what he had in mind. He knew he was going to get a response, because they were in the same situation as he was. They were all for it. Young Curtis said he could get a guitar from his other uncle, who was lying in a gully on the other side of the line. Lucky bugger, thought Charlie.

Young Curtis didn't take long to get back with the guitar, thus putting the plan into motion. He and old Uncle had heard *My Boomerang Won't Come Back* before and liked it, but they didn't know the words. "I know the tune," Charlie told them. "Use your own Wongi words, swear at 'em if you want, just as long as it's in tune with the song and in the Wongi lingo."

They practised for a while until Charlie was satisfied. He couldn't understand the words and didn't give a shit. As long as they were in tune with the song, that's all that mattered. Young Curtis told him a pub across from the railway station might listen to them, but Charlie would have to do the talkin'.

"No worries," said Charlie, "that's right up my alley. I can talk a snake into biting itself. Come on, let's move," he said, thinking of the departure of the train.

When they got there, Charlie told them to wait outside while he went in and talked to the boss. After a while he came out and told them to come inside. They were a bit hesitant while first standing at the bar but, once the barman bought them a double port each, they soon relaxed.

"Right, you two," said Charlie ordering another and gulping it down. "The boss said if you two can make 'em piss, you'll have all the gerbah out, and he'll give you money on top of it." This seemed to relax them even more. A couple more and they'd sing in Buckingham Palace, with no coaxing, thought Charlie, eyeing them as they gulped their drinks down.

The boss came over to Charlie and asked if his boys were ready to start, and could he give them an introduction to the people.

"Okay, boss," he said, as he made his way to the stage. Shit, I haven't given them a name yet, he thought as he grabbed for the mike. "Hello, ladies and gentlemen, I'm about to introduce you to the singing duet. They are called "The Boomerangs" and I can guarantee if you threw these boomerangs away, they'll always come back. Just ask the coppers," which brought a roar of laughter from the crowd. "They have performed in various missions in the outback, also in Alice Springs and Darwin, where they had the top billing among such performers as Bob Hawk, John Howard, Bruce Ruxton, Michael Mansell and Jo Bjelke-Peterson," which brought a louder cheer from the audience who were all white people.

"Please, ladies and gentlemen, they will be singing in their own language, so don't bother to understand the words. The song they're going to perform is a Charlie Drake number. It's called My *Boomerang Won't Come Back*, which got the crowd laughing and jeering as Charlie beckoned them up.

"Right, you two," he whispered in their ears,

"Make 'em piss but stay in tune." As he left the stage, Curtis started to strum, then sing, joined by Uncle. Charlie became aware of the crowd beginning to take notice. The boss came over with a drink for him.

"Here, mate," he said.

"Thanks," said Charlie, "they okay?"

"Yeah," said the boss, "how long have they been together?"

"Six, eight months or more," said Charlie, as they finished their song. The crowd was yelling for more and Charlie could see Uncle and Curtis were badly in need of a drink. He whispered to the boss, who told the barman to take a jug of beer up to the performers. Good, thought Charlie, as he noticed them gulping the beer down, drinking beer won't get them pissed as quick.

They started again, which got the crowd clapping. Either these two are natural born performers, thought Charlie, scratching his head, or these white people have never heard two full-blooded Wongis perform before. One's over sixty and the other about twenty. I must have a gift for finding natural performers. I must have. He switched to beer and enjoyed his middie, grinning with glee as people came up to give him money for his performers.

The boss came over and asked Charlie if he could understand them. "Of course!" he said with dignity. "They can't sing in English, only in their own language. And I can understand every word they say."

The boss gave him a handful of dollar bills, saying, "I hope their schedule isn't too hectic. I'd like to have them back once in a while."

Charlie nearly burst out laughing, for he felt like telling him that the whole tribe just camped outside his back yard in the lanes. But getting back into a business-like manner said, "I haven't checked yet, but I'll let you know."

"Good," said the boss shaking his hand.

The more jugs of beer they got, the more they performed. Not only Charlie Drake's song, but Slim Dusty, Charlie Pride and a few Christian hymns for good measure. Always in their own lingo. They must have been going for a couple of hours or more, before chucking it in. A good thing too, thought Charlie, they're getting too pissed. At one stage, they tried to sing the national anthem in English. Charlie waved them to him, much to the annoyance of the crowd who gave them a standing ovation.

"Well, you blokes made 'em piss alright," said Charlie, as he led them outside. "Here, take this," giving them a handful of dollar bills. "There's enough money here to keep the tribe drunk and on kangaroo tails for a week. And you deserve it," he said shaking their hands.

"Where you going now?" asked Curtis.

"To catch that train home to Perth," said Charlie, pointing across to the station.

As he made his way to the station, he suddenly stopped in his tracks and called back to Curtis,

"What was the words youse were using to sing to the people in the pub?"

"Go to the shithouse and stick a spear up your bum!" shouted Curtis as he and Uncle staggered off to some lane.

Fifteen

Uncle Jacko

"Brickwall Oswald Jackson," shouted the local sergeant to a group of Nyoongars standing around outside the courthouse, waiting to appear before the justice of the peace. The Nyoongars were mainly charged with execrable offences, such as drunk and disorderly, being on licensed premises, using obscene language and, if the police were lucky, drunk driving. The Nyoongars shouted cruel when they heard what the Sarge called Uncle Jacko.

"More like Brickwall Bigballs Jackson" . . . "dus a poxy name, Uncle Jacko," . . . "dus your real name, Uncle Jacko?" they were laughing.

Um gunna show these little piss arses, thought the seventy two year old, dignified Aboriginal man striding purposely towards the court, neatly attired in his five dollar fifty op-shop suit. He approached the sergeant who acknowledged him and said, "You know what to do and say."

After thirty minutes or more Uncle Jacko strode out and stood on the steps, extended his arms out and addressed his multitude. He said, in a loud clear voice, "For the nine-hundred-and ninety-ninth time, Brickwall Oswald Jackson, I have no alternative but to caution you for being drunk on public property."

All the Nyoongars shouted and clapped. He heard cries of, "Moorditj, Uncle Jacko," . . . "Made 'em piss, Uncle Jacko," . . . "Nearly thousan', Uncle Jacko," . . . "You deadly, Uncle Jacko."

He walked away from the courthouse, punching the air with a little skip and hearing the Sarge call out to the multitude of Nyoongars, "Quiet, please, court's in session."

"You mob lucky, orright. If you mob back in da ol' days, ol' JP would give you a month in Fremantle Prison, jus' for drunk. 'Course I know, I bin Fremantle," Uncle Jacko chuckled, making his way to Flo's house. He knew why they had picked him up. It all started when he was asleep under a shrub, in a vacant block. He hadn't been able to make it to Topsy's place as he was too drunk and so he decided to have a rest, eventually going off to sleep, until that munartj shone a torch in his face saying, "Come on, Jacko, to the cell you go."

That one little sleep cost him a muntj. He cursed himself rigorously before jumping in that rat van. Never mind, he thought, Topsy still got 'im with her, never sold it to anyone. I hope not, chuckling to himself, walking head down.

"What you smilin' 'bout?" scowled Flo, bringing him back to now and today. "I heard all 'bout you," she continued, "'magine you ol' buntji man, sleepin' under bush. Choo, shame."

He realized he was outside of Flo's house. He hadn't seen or spoken to any Nyoongars since he left the courthouse, yet she knew exactly what happened. Gawd, what dis woman, ghost, devil or what? he thought. Then he asked her, "How you know what happen'?"

"Yarns be told before you do it. You know dis little town, fulla Nyoongars."

Dat tore it, he thought, shaking his head.

"Come for cuppa tea, Brickwall da Beast," she said, laughing.

"Gawd, I bin not hearin' dat name for a long time," he said, laughing along with her. He remembered how Toby gave him that name before he took off to Leonora.

"Hear from Toby?" he asked, sipping his tea. Not the liquid required at the moment, he thought, but dis will do.

"Naw, not even Brenda," she said, feeling angry with both, but especially with Toby.

"Never mind, he get welfare to tell you he orright," he said hopefully. Although he wasn't related to him, Uncle Jacko really liked Toby and admired him. Uncle Jacko could see that Toby was going to make it to the top. Whenever Toby knew Uncle Jacko was in jail, he was always there to bail him out. Every time he'd bail him out, he'd say, "Come on, Brickwall the Beast, you got no shame. Promising all these old yorgahs a muntj last night. They reckon there were five old yorgahs waitin' on you. You want that big beast of yours cut off." Then they'd both walk down to the pub laughing. Toby had a kind, caring, forgiving way that everybody loved. But poor boy, he thought, some day he will learn to love in return.

"Who tell 'em you 'bout me, anyway?" he asked, forgetting about Toby.

Flo laughed at Uncle Jacko and being a good strong Christian lady, told him in a gracious manner exactly how she was told. "Dey reckon you was layin' down, tryin' to do dirty to the sand."

"What," he spluttered, nearly swallowing the big mug of tea.

"Dus not all, you had your trousers down 'round your ankles," she said laughing, "An' dat munartj was shinin' da torch on your bare ring," she added, going into fits of laughter.

"Don't you talk 'bout me like dat, Florence," he said, getting up from the table, clenching his jaw and fists at the same time.

"Dus other Nyoongars . . . "

"Fuck da other Nyoongars," he shouted angrily, cutting Flo off in mid sentence.

Regaining her composure, she said, "Don't you swear in dis house. Dis is da Lord's house, you know um a Christian. I like my Church."

That really spun Uncle Jacko out. His anger went into overdrive, his blood pressure went through the roof. Flames seemed to come out of his mouth and nostrils . . . he was seething. His growl not that of a human being, "You tell me who said dat yarn to you. 'Cause um gonna skittle da first Nyoongar who look at me." He continued growling and throwing a combination of left and right jabs. Flo was still laughing at Uncle Jacko's antics and managing to subdue him. Settling down on the chair, he said "Choo, you know these Nyoongars. Gunna stretch that yarn cruel."

Flo shook her head and said, "What for you bein' silly?"

Gawd, thought Uncle Jacko, if she don't believe me, these other Nyoongars won't. Dat yarn already gone around Australia while um sittin' here.

"I know these Nyoongars, dey like stretchin' 'em," she said smiling. Uncle Jacko went on to tell her exactly what happened, why he got picked up and why he was charged for sleeping under that bush.

"Dat gerbah no good for you. Gib it away. Be a Christian like me and come to church," she said.

Gawd, dus all I need right now, he thought. "No, um orright. Um doin' some paintin' now," he said, getting her on side.

"Yeah, dey bin tellin' me you bin doin' some paintin'. Dat flash watjella you talk to, dey reckon he gotta flash car too," she said.

Uncle Jacko adjusted his tie, brushed back his long silver-grey hair and said with some authority, "Dat flash car, dey call him Lambro something,"

"What dus a I . . . talian man, unna?" she asked.

"No," he shouted, "Dus da name of his flash car."

"Don't have to shout," she said sternly.

"Um sorry, Flo, dis yarn make me feel no good. But something big gonna happen to me," he said seriously.

"Only thing big gunna happen, if you come to church. Give your heart to the Lord," she said, hoping to break through that armour of sin.

Dis woman don't give up, he thought. In a more serious manner, he told her of his talent, found in a cell whilst waiting to go to court for drunk and disorderly. Toby wasn't there to bail him out, so he asked the old Sarge for some paint and paper. He had three hours to kill, so he did some paintings. When the Sarge saw the paintings, he was very impressed with Uncle Jacko's work. He kept them, saying he would pass them on to this art dealer he knew in Perth. He had done some more paintings and the art dealer himself was very impressed. He encouraged Uncle Jacko to keep working at his art and had taken his paintings overseas. Even the world was impressed with his work, his dot paintings, saturated with Aboriginal culture and stories, going back thousands of years.

"So you see, I bin painting on da quiet. I don't want these other Nyoongars to know what um doin'. Dus why I got off with a caution. Ol' Sarge tell 'em JP I might be goin' overseas soon," he said with renewed vigour in his voice.

Flo looked at Uncle Jacko in awe, No, not dis ol' buntji man. Why, he only drunken ol' sinner, she thought.

"Look, Florence, um seventy two now. Come next rain I be seventy three," he said, feeling very proud of himself for living so long. A lot of his relations and friends did not reach the age of sixty. Sometimes younger, he thought, dat stinkin' gerbah kill 'em all. Then saying with meaning, "Yeah, Florence, I want dis world to know who Brickwall Oswald Jackson is before he die."

"What, you keep drinkin' dat flagon, you be finished. Only us fullahs here know you, dus all," she said.

"Yeah, dus what I bin thinkin'," he said solemnly.

"Yeah, be good if ol' sister bin livin' today. She be proud of you," she said, feeling sad for Eunice.

"Yeah," he said, thinking of all the good times he and Eunice had together. But he knew their Aboriginal custom was not to speak of the dead and he and Flo respected this wholeheartedly.

"You know dis watjella, he comin' 'round here," he said to Flo.

"Where, here?" she asked.

"Here, right here," he said indicating her house.

"What for you tell 'em to come here?" she snapped.

"Course um not gunna tell him to pick me up under some bush," he said laughing.

"Choo, you got no shame tellin' 'im to come to my place. What, he comin' in his flash car?" she asked.

"Course, what you think, he comin' in a horse and cart," he said, laughing. He could see that Flo was looking at him in a different way from an old drunken buntji man sinner.

"When he comin', today?" she asked.

"Any time now, soon be today," he told her.

"Choo, I gotta clean my place up," she said nervously.

"Don't worry, Florence, dis house cleana den da Buckingham Palace where da Queen lives," he said laughing.

"Yeah, Brickwall, if you see her over there, you'll be asking her to have a drink from your flagon," she laughed and called him a buntji man.

"Ni, ni, motor pulled up outside, unna?" he asked.

"Yeah, dus him," she said.

Flo and Uncle Jacko rushed to the front door to see a gleaming red Lamborghini parked outside her house. She couldn't get over how the door was opened from the inside and lifted straight up like the top of the car was holding the door up like a big eagle with one wing lifted up. A well-dressed man got out and Uncle Jacko approached him smiling.

"Mr Jackson, nice to see you again," he said

"Call me Jacko an' what your name again?" he asked.

"Mario, Mario Muntjama," he told him.

"Oh, yeah, dus right. Look, I want you to meet my ol' friend," he said, nodding towards Flo who was standing on the verandah.

She couldn't believe what she saw. A flash car, looking like it came from outer space, and a man with over a thousand dollars worth of suit on and all those gold trinkets hanging off him. He was standing there shaking hands with Uncle Jacko in his five dollar fifty op-shop suit. No, she thought, Dis mus' be a dream, as she watched Uncle Jacko and the man approach her.

"Flo, meet dis here Mario," he said, introducing them with a smug smile on his face. He could see Nyoongars along the street, peeping out of their yards. They couldn't believe what they were seeing. Flo and Mario acknowledged each other. Then Mario turned to Uncle Jacko and said "You'll have to come to Perth with me, then we fly off to America."

Uncle Jacko went into the staggers, grabbing his chest with his mouth open, but no words coming out while Flo grabbed the verandah post for support. She, too, was in a state of collapse.

"I am sorry, I should have told you while you were sitting down," he said, grabbing Uncle Jacko to support him.

Regaining his composure, Jacko's words came flowing free, "What you talkin' 'bout 'merica for?"

he asked, wanting Mario to repeat himself.

"'merica, 'merica, what you gunna do there," Flo asked, getting over her shock.

Mario did repeat his words, but not before making sure Uncle Jacko and Flo were in a stable position on the chairs. He told them he had arranged an exhibition at the Museum of Contemporary Art in New York City. The leading painters from America and Europe were very impressed with Uncle Jacko's work and, above all, they wanted Uncle Jacko to be there in person at the Museum of Contemporary Art in New York City, America.

"Ol' man like me, Brickwall Oswald Jackson, goin' 'merica, seventy two years old, I be blowed, ay," he said in a trance.

"Those paintings are of your wonderful culture, the world is eager to know of your work and your culture," said Mario, sounding very impressive.

"Um gunna tell Toby an' all these other Nyoongars here dat you gunna be big shot," said Flo, coming to her senses.

"The money you make over there, Mr Jackson, you'll be able to buy your own country town," said Mario, spinning Uncle Jacko out.

"How um goin' again?" he asked.

"We'll be flying first class, but you'll have to stay at the Hyatt Regency, a big hotel in Perth, and your passport is all fixed up. You'll have to get a new wardrobe, then we're off," Mario told him.

"What wardrobe?" he asked, wondering what

he was going to do walking around with a wardrobe on his back in the middle of Perth.

"You know, new clothes, a suit," Mario said, "But you are not to worry about a thing. I'll fix all that up," he added.

"What you call dat car?" asked Flo, pointing to his car.

"Lamborghini. Mr Jackson could have one too if this exhibition is succesful, as no doubt I know it will be," said Mario.

"What, we goin' now?" asked Uncle Jacko, still in a daze.

"Yes, we've got to be in Perth soon," he said

"C'mon, den," he said, hugging and kissing Flo. Then he headed towards the car. The last words Uncle Jacko heard from Flo, before disappearing from the town, were "'member me, when you be big shot."

Sixteen

The Last Plot

Drowsing in the warm sun, a gentle breeze stirred at his thoughts and he smiled to himself. I mus' be goin' mad, he thought, fancy me, a man of learning and a good Catholic upbringing . . . Why . . . did I have to muntj that old watjella yorgah las' night! Gawd, she mus' be fifteen stone or more, an' me only eight stone. I musta looked like a rabbit tryin' to muntj a elephant, he thought, cackling to himself. But da wors' part after I muntjed her, I stole her bottle of plonk and when I walked out her back door, I kicked da piss outta her little poxy dawg. Holy fuck! going into fits of uncontrollable laughter. "Gotta stop dis laughin' too much, makin' gobberl warra," he scolded himself harshly while trying to control his laughter.

Getting up slowly and holding his stomach with a great degree of care and not wanting to laugh any more, he changed his thoughts to the here and now. I hope those two ol' boys hurry up. He came from out of the bushes to peer towards town, scratching his head. At the ripe old age of seventy two, Old Yonga Yallop, as everybody in town called him, was a proper old buntji man. Indeed, he would respond with a smile and a twinkle in his eye, basking in his notoriety.

The older Nyoongars, who had passed on, reckoned his rightful name was Yanbi Yallop, but old Yonga couldn't come to terms with his rightful name. Some of the elders said the name in Nyoongar meant 'awkward', 'improper' and 'incorrect'. Of course, it was quite the opposite to his given name, plus the fact the Nyoongars would throw in 'yandi', 'gunja', 'pot', 'weed', 'dope' or 'grass', all names stemming from the drug marijuana. Old Yonga Yallop had never smoked anything legal or illegal in his seventy two years of life. He just liked his gerbah.

The reason the Nyoongars called him Yonga was that every time you'd go around to Yonga's flat, he'd be cooking a big feed of kangaroo meat and always had a big hot damper on the side, cooling. Hence the name, Yonga, which the Nyoongars called a kangaroo. Every time he'd come into contact with other Nyoongars, he'd ask for the price of a bottle of plonk and, in the same breath, say, "Got any yonga meat?" He'd even asked the watjellas around town. Some would give him money, but when he asked for yonga meat, he had them bewildered. The expressions on their faces said they didn't understand and he'd walk away, saying, "Neber mine, den, I go an' ask a Nyoongar." You see, old Yonga was partially deaf and he'd only hear what he wanted to hear, or so his two old mate's would say. So 'Yonga' it was.

Old Willie Walljun, also known to the town Nyoongars as 'Willie Willie', 'Willie Wagtail', 'Chitti Chitti', 'Walljup' or even 'the Big W', which had no bearing on his looks. In fact, he was short and fat with predominantly Aboriginal features. It didn't bother him what they called him as long as they had gerbah on them. He, too, was a sixty nine year old buntji man, as the old yorgahs who lived in the pensioners' flats, often called him.

Yonga's other friend was the equally virile seventy year Billy Brundle, or as the Nyoongars who know him would call him 'Boyyah Billy Brundle'. Those who didn't know him would call him that behind his back or they'd say Big Balls Boyyah Billy Brundle. They'd never call him that to his face, though. The Nyoongars had a knack of turning a given name into a humorous nick name. Talk about being creative in literature. Even Shakespeare, himself, would envy their creativeness. However, every time Billy Brundle would see a Nyoongar, he'd say "boyyah wa," which means 'any money'? Or there abouts. Nevertheless, those words were used mainly on off-pension week by himself, along with his other two old cobbers.

The other Nyoongars would make a detour from the on-coming, three old mates. If caught unaware, old Boyyah's initial impact would be "boyyah wa," as he stood there, hand outstretched, his old grey eyes looking downcast in forlorn hope. His other two old mates would adopt that pose and mumble, "Gee, we crook, cruel," visibly shaking almost beyond redemption. The Nyoongars that old Boyyah asked would look at them with sympathetic eyes and heart. If they got any money, they would give openly and say, "Here, go an' get a flagon." If they didn't have any, they would say, "Noorn, we got nothing, dear ol' uncles . . . but . . . " When the three old boys heard the word, 'but', their ears would prick up and they knew that some Nyoongar, somewhere, had some money.

"Simmo gottem cheque today, ask him, he gib you." The three old blokes would profoundly acknowledge their saviours and go in search of Simmo in eager anticipation, almost tasting the sweet wine on their lips. With undue haste, they walked past the butcher shop. Looking in the window while moving away, they almost bumped into Simmo who was coming out of the deli.

"Choo, where my ol' uncles runnin' to?" Grabbing onto them to steady them so they didn't fall over each other, Simmo looked at them in a quizzical way before saying, "What, you three been muntjin' all night or what? 'Cause you three look fucked," laughing at the three desperadoes in front of him. He heard the familiar words 'boyyah wa', which he was expecting. Between laughs, he managed to splutter, "Oh, gawd, how I know what you mob want." Regaining his composure and rummaging inside his pockets, his fingers came upon a note – the one that he hoped it would be – and pulling it out slowly, he'd hold it out to them, saying, "Now, here's twenty dollars for you old kids; dis oughta stop the shakes." Three arms snapped at a ferocious speed towards the note and Simmo, who anticipated their every move, quickly stepped back. This made the three lunge into his girth, almost knocking him over. Regaining his balance quickly and laughing, he steadied them down. He didn't want to see a tangle of arms and legs on the street. These three old blokes would have difficulties standing upright plus the fact that three heart attacks all at once was quite natural, given the condition they were in.

"Noorn, my three old uncles mus' be dyin' for a charge," he said to them in a sombre mood.

"Course, we feel warra an' no gnumerries, too," responded Boyyah rather quickly.

"Okay, den, here's twenty bucks for your gerbah an' ten for your gnumerries an' don't let these youn' fella's cadge you three old blokes," Simmo said sternly.

"No. No way," they said in unison.

"Here, den," passing the money over and saying, "You mob gotta gib ten dollars each on pension day, if not um gonna get some big yorgah to drag you three all aroun' dis town by your yortjs," which got them all laughing.

Yeah, thought Yonga, Simmo dead now, what dey reckon was a heart attack or something an' only at fifty one. Dese Nyoongars finished today. Get to fifty an' dey gone, me Boyyah an' Willie all pas' dat now. But we still like our gerbah an' yorgahs, laughing to himself. Going back to the bushes and finding his favourite log to sit on, his thoughts went back to when the wheat and sheep town of Nona was thriving. Fat wool and wheat cheques were a common occurrence. The shire council was healthy with workers, the water supply had a healthy body of workers and the farmers would come right to your door step to pick you up for work. Nyoongars were in abundance and so was work. Now in this rural town, lean years were growing rapidly. Many of the people, both Nyoongars and watjellas had gradually left for the city. There were a few Nyoongars around, not many though. The only prized possession left was the bush the three old boys drank in.

It wasn't that far from town, about a half hour's walk and it was a cover for the three old boys with their gerbah. To sit, drink and yarn was good, especially away from the munartjs' prying eyes. The three old boys did not like some of those crazy Nyoongars in town, who insisted on swearing and fighting each other right outside the pub. It was no place for the three old boys to be. These few acres left was their haven and depending on whether the weather was cool or cold, they would make a fire and old Yonga would always bring his kangaroo meat to roast. They would drink, eat and keep warm and, depending how inebriated they were, quite often they would sleep around the fire with the wind and the bushes gently humming to them. If it was a windy night, the bushes would scream out their anger against the developers because there was no protection from large trees or forest; only cleared farming land as far as the horizon and beyond. First light would be their alarm clock, well before the sun glared it's teeth on the three lonely figures sipping their wine and roasting their meat in the midst of their little island of bush paradise. They'd often say to each other while charging on, "If um gonna die, bury me right here," stubbing the soil with their feet.

"'Cause dis here little bit ob land is our las' plot. Nobody can take him 'way from us, unna," said old Yonga passionately.

"Yeah, dis true, my gnoonie," shouted old Boyyah and Willie, with equal passion. Yeah, thought Yonga, we bin drinkin' 'ere lawng time now. Dere was a lotta trees 'round den. Now da crops come closer and closer; nex' time dere be nothing. Dis little bush lef' now, I bin 'member 'im when we had our first gerbah an' we call 'im Yonga's, Boyyah's an' Willies' acres. Now we gotta call 'im, Willie, Yonga and Boyyah's little acre. Watching a lizard scurrying past his feet, he said, rather sorrowfully, to the lizard, "You be soon like me, nowhere to hide. We jus' gotta find somewhere, but where? Soon dere be no more bushes to hide in," watching the lizard scamper down a hole.

"You right now to hide, but not for long. Soon, my little friend, ol' Yonga be like you, will go in da groun' inna a coffin, only spirit will come back," said Yonga, brushing a tear away from his eye.

Old Yonga was deep in thought, occasionally stirring to look at a bird that landed on a branch not far from him and he'd smile and think, noorn, poor little fella, mus' be tired an' stop for rest before flyin' on to da big bush were he belong. Old Yonga, Willie and Boyyah felt deep in their hearts that this bit of bush left was doomed to make way for progress, but they never spoke of it outwardly. To them, it was theirs.

Their ancestors roamed this beautiful forest from day one, long before fences were put up to make the paddocks suitable for wheat crops, and sheep, cattle and horses grazing on watjellas land being disturbed by intruders. The Aborigines (the intruders) speared their stock to supplement their diet as the kangaroos, like the Aborigines, were driven further and further away. Both were dispossessed of the freedom to roam at will. They were both in the same situation. The kangaroo being speared for food or shot as vermin by the farmer, whilst the Aborigines were shot for spearing sheep or cattle or had their drinking holes poisoned. Both were regarded as pests by the early settlers of that other country.

Dese two should be comin', Yonga thought hopefully. Getting up and walking to the edge of his resort, he peered towards town and noticed his two old mates coming towards him. Both smoking and heavily laden with gerbah. Das good, he thought, dey gottem gerbah an' gnumerries. Dey mus' be habbem meat, too. I get um fire ready.

Feeling pleased with himself, he gathered a few sticks up and put them on the embers and stirred it up with small twigs. Sitting on his favourite log, he watched the embers give birth to flames. It was a pleasant day and the fire was irrelevant, but if they got meat, regardless of the day, a fire was essential. He heard them coming towards him, laughing, joking and behaving like two kangaroos with their tails cut off.

"We gottem two casks of Moselle an' two packet gnumerries," shouted Boyyah rather pleased with his efforts.

"You gettem meat," responded Yonga almost instantaneously.

"You think we cartwarra or what? Course we gottem meat, you know we always bring um back. Here, look in dis," was Boyyah's retort as he placed the bag at his feet, which annoyed Willie who, being the youngest of the trio, had always placed the responsibility on himself to look after the tucker department. Yonga knew this and it always irritated Willie when asked that question.

"Come on, den, open a cask," said Yonga, grabbing his cup, which he always had next to the log. "Ah, good, you got some namesake meat an' some mutton flaps," Yonga said with glee.

"Course," said Willie feeling pleased with himself, because Yonga was pleased. Sometimes old Yonga could become quite irrational if Willie had forgotten about the meat and it took about four cups of wine to get him back in the right frame of mind. “Here, den,” said Willie, passing Yonga his cup and filling Boyyah’s cup and passing it on to him. He, then, proceeded to top up his own cup.

The cups they had weren’t the cups you’d drink daintily from and talk about the latest stock market results, or enquire about the equestrian events in a noble manner. No, these cups, as the three old boys called them, were actually jam tins, cleaned up and used time and time again. They had about two cans each and if one had the others’ cups by sheer eagerness for a drink, or just by pure mistake, they’d actually come near to blows.

“Ahh, dus good,” said Yonga, wiping his mouth with the back of his hand and feeling the alcohol hitting the pit of his stomach and sending shock waves through his entire body.

“Too true, my gnoon,” responded Boyyah.

“Dat settlin’ me right down,” was Willie’s reply.

“Anyway, where youse get all dis from?” asked Yonga.

“Hang on, I tell you all. Let me top my cup up first,” replied Boyyah, finishing the last that was left in his can before filling it up again. Willie and Yonga did likewise and sat back on their logs, ears open and eyes twinkling.

“It was like dis; I run into Nora an’ I was talkin’ to her an’ she as’ me where you.”

“Who, me?” asked Yonga

“Yeah, you,” replied Willie. “Stop buttin’ in an’ let him finish,” he said sternly. “I might get a muntj, unna," which got both Willie and Boyyah laughing.

"Anyway," said Boyyah, "I was talkin' to Nora an' she said it was 'dowment day today an' her daughter got hers an' you can see all da kids runnin' round with pies, ice cream, lollies an' cool drinks. Dey look like dey was eatin' a pie, ice cream an' lollies all at once. So I as' Nora an' she gimme fifteen dollars an' some gnumeeries."

"Yeah, dus true, I was dere" chimed in Willie.

"Goorn, den tell dis yarn," snapped Yonga. "An' keep quiet, Willie Willie." Yonga was eager to hear this yarn and there might be a couple of yorgahs stung up.

"Yeah, me an' Boyyah know what you thinkin', you only think of your yortj," said Willie laughing, which got them all laughing together.

Managing to subdue his laughter, Boyyah said, "Yeah, anyway, after I lef' Nora, me an' Big W run into Topsy an' her daughter who got paid. Her grannies, dey was runnin' 'round with the shop in dere hands. One little fella had roller skates in one 'and an' a bike in der other. Anyway, I bin talkin' to Topsy an' she gib me twenty dollar and some more gnumeeries. So me an' Big W was right. An' we walkin' to da pub an' we run into Daisy an' her daughter got um 'dowment. I cadged her for twenty dollars an' she gib me an' some more gnumeeries. Dere was a few Nyoongars in da pub an' dey 'ad dat juke box fairly pissin'. Dey was makin' Charlie Pride an' Slim Dusty yodel wicked. When I got da gerbah, one youn'

Nyoongar, only young fucker, shouted out to me, 'Hey, Big Balls Boyyah Billy Brundle.' Don't know who da fuck he is. Anyway, dey only fuckin' blow-in's. I wish I was younger, I woulda knock him right on his hole." With the help of the gerbah, old Boyyah got up, unsteady, of course.

He got into boxer's stance and started to throw a combination of left and right jabs to his imaginary opponent, which got Yonga and Willie shouting encouragement.

"Goorn, jab 'im again, goorn knock 'im out, you makin' him piss, rip 'im, rip right up 'im, you got 'im fucked now, go in for the kill, brother." Dust was swirling around Boyyah, when he decided on the last knockout punch to his imaginary opponent.

Willie shouted, "Goorn, Big Balls, make 'im piss in da air."

Extracting his last ounce of strength, Boyyah threw a mighty left upper-cut which lifted himself right off his feet. It wasn't planned this way, but by being in the air, he lost his balance and landed flat on his back. Yonga and Willie had ringside seats and were very quiet. There was a look of concern on their faces. Waiting for the dust to settle so they could get a glimpse of their hero, they saw see him move on the ground among the dust. They shouted and clapped. Rolling onto his right elbow and looking directly at his two fans, who were practically wetting themselves from laughing, he wiped the dust from his eyes and said, "Did I knock 'im out or what?"

That brought tears to Yonga and Willie's eyes, before Willie, who managed to control his laughing for a few minutes, said, "I be fucked, aye, dus the first time I see a Nyoongar knock 'imself out."

Well, the laughter that erupted from the bush by Yonga, Boyyah and Willie. They reckon it was the noise of terrified dingo pups who had been abandoned by their mother at birth. The towns' folk say the wind brings that sound back to that particular spot on lonely dark nights.

The three old blokes got up and gingerly walked around, not daring to look at each other as they managed to regain their composure with great difficulty.

"Fill 'im cup up for me, Willie, an' throw some namesake meat on da coals," said Yonga. Willie did this obligingly and filled up Boyyah's cup which he passed to both, before putting some yonga meat on the coals. Boyyah, who dusted his clothes with a smirk on his face, grabbed his cup and sat down on his log.

"Well," said Yonga, trying not laugh, "dus was da bes' fight I ebber seen."

"No more talkin' 'bout dat fight, my gobberl no good, laughin' too much," said Boyyah rubbing his stomach.

"Mine same too," replied Willie.

"Yeah, um gonna hab a good feed ob namesake meat an' good drink den hab a rest. Bin feelin' little tired lately an' Boyyah fighten' 'imself an' me laughin' too much, made me feel warra," said Yonga more or less to himself.

"Yeah, you charge up an' hab a good feed," said Boyyah.

"Here, your namesake meat cooked, hab a good feed," said Willie with concern. They all sat around and had a good old yarn and, of course, a good old feed. Talking mainly about Nyoongars and the main topic was tuppies and muntj or muntj and tuppies, the occasional fight was thrown in and gerbah.

"I go lay down," Yonga said. Stretching himself before grabbing some leaves for a mattress and small size rock for a pillow. Lying down in the warm sun, he was soon drowsing and hearing voices from the past.

"You reckon he be right," asked Willie looking down at Yonga. "Course, he madda iron, him. Let barrl sleep."

"Yeah, okay, den," responded Willie. They continued their drinking and clean up the last of the kangaroo meat that was left and Boyyah saying,

"Yeah, Big W. I wonder if dis bush be still 'ere when we dead an' gone?" Looking at the last bit of bush left that connected them to the soil.

"Yeah, I hope so. Other youn' one's can come up 'ere, hab a good drink, a good muntj an' a good fuckin' fight," which got them both laughin', thinking of the days when the bush around was thick and all the fights and muntj's they had, but mostly the muntj's.

"Yeah," Boyyah said, "dere plenty ob yorgahs on dere backs here." Both laughing. "Ni, Ni, motor car pull up, might be 'lations. Go an' hab a look,

Willie". Willie got up and took a peek through the bushes.

"Hey, fuckin' munartj here, hide da drink," said Willie nervously.

"Dey bin seen us drinkin' here before. Fuck da munartjs," said Boyyah aggressively.

The sergeant and his constable came into the clearing and looked over and around the camp site. "I thought I'd find you here," said the Sarge.

"You know us, we bin just drinkin', Sarge. We cause no trouble." said a suspicious Boyyah.

"Of course, I know that, you three are the least of my problems. Old Yonga sleep, I see," said the Sarge. They both nodded and waited on what he was going to say next, but the young constable took on the talking, saying,

"I'm afraid you three, by law, cannot come up here and drink anymore." That was a kick in the guts to them.

"What you talkin' 'bout," Boyyah sneered at him.

"I'm sorry," said the Sarge, "the council has taken over this bit of land . . . and they are going to clear it. They had a council meeting last night and it has been approved for redevelopment purposes."

"Now, dus not fair, we bin drinkin' 'ere for twenty years or more. Dey can't take dis from us," Willie pleaded.

"Look, Willie, I don't want to get into a debate, we could be here all afternoon. I suggest you go and wake old Yonga and we'll give you a lift back to town," said the Sarge, really feeling for the three old gentlemen.

"Hey, hey, Sarge, we can't wake him up," cried Willie in a shrill voice. The sergeant nodded to his constable to check old Yonga out. He felt for a pulse; there was none. Looking at the young constable's face, the Sarge knew he was dead. He walked over to Willie and Boyyah to tell them their old mate was dead. Willie and Boyyah were standing looking at dear old Yonga when the sergeant approached them.

"I'm sorry he's . . . "

"Yeah, we know," said Willie taking off his coat and covering old Yonga's head. He put his arm around Boyyah's shoulder as they both looked down on the lifeless body.

Boyyah said, "Good-bye, my ol' ngoonie. You died where you belong, in our las' plot, but you can't be buried here 'cause council take um away. Neber mind, den, you hadda good drink an' a good feed ob your namesake meat," wiping a tear from his eye. Looking at Willie, he said, "You wanna say anything to ol' Yonga?"

Shaking his head, Willie said, "You said it all, my brother."

"Excuse me," said the Sarge, "the ambulance is here."

They watched the body of old Yonga being placed on a stretcher. After giving Willie his coat back, they covered Yonga with a sheet and placed him in the back of the ambulance, shutting the door. Willie and Boyyah walked back to the police van with the sergeant and his constable. The sergeant opened the back door and said, "Where do you want to be let off?"

"To the pensioners flat," said Willie. Just before the Sarge closed the door, old Boyyah asked him, "What dey gunna build here?"

"A swimming pool," he said, closing the door.

Seventeen

The Law Breaker

Topsy knew she was breaking the law when she gave birth to two babies. The missionaries at Kalgoorlie were concerned for the safety of the little fair one and put him up for adoption at the time.

In the old tribal law, if a woman gave birth to more than one child, it was wrong. She was allowed to keep only one. She'd had a one night drunken fling with a white man and the end result were two beautiful baby boys; one as black as the night itself, the other, the colour of a brand new day dawning.

Before he was due to be taken away by the white family, she asked the nurse to bring the fair one to her. She knew she was disobeying her customs but, after all, she was the mother and she loved this little fair one as much as she loved the little black one. When the nurse brought the fair one to her, she cradled him to her heart and a great flood of tears cascaded down her cheeks.

She said to him in her native tongue, "Go away, my little fair one, for my heart and spirit will travel with you. I do not wish to let you go but it's the law of our people. You didn't want to come into this world. It is I who made our ancestors angry. Now it is I whose heart will bleed for my little fair one. I am going to give you my spirit. If anything is wrong with me or our tribe, you will see a wise old owl. No one else will see it, only you."

As she rubbed the palm of her hand all over his little sleeping body, she could feel him moving under her touch, beginning to stir, then she started to sing in a low haunting voice. The wailing woke the little one who opened his eyes and looked straight into his mother's face. She said to him in a small voice, "You have got two spirits now, my little one. I have nothing, for I will slowly die as you get bigger and stronger. I am like a shell you pick up on the sea shore. Nothing left inside. As the rain and the sun comes, the shell will crumble to dust. The winds will come and blow the dust over our hunting grounds. The shell might see the next rain. Then nothing."

Topsy squeezed the little one onto her chest. They were both crying when the nurse rushed in. She stopped in her tracks as she looked at the sight of mother and baby. She, too, nearly burst out crying. It reminded her of a story a Sunday school teacher told her when she was a child; the story was being played right before her eyes, only the words were different. The mother was looking into heaven, while the baby was screaming its lungs out, and she was shouting out, "Don't let him be crucified, let him help his people. Alcohol is killing our people and their minds; let this little one rise above it all and bring our people back to their culture. Within him are two spirits, let them guide him on the right path, and I know my dust will go back to the soil."

They both went quiet as if by command. This is unnatural, thought the nurse, as she stood frozen to the floor, wiping the tears from her eyes. A strange sensation seemed to take over the room. She wanted to turn and run, but she felt as if something was holding her there against her will, making sure she witnessed this unexplained situ ation. There was a breeze blowing straight at mother and baby, but not strong enough to rustle the curtains, just their hair and the bed linen. The air ventilation isn't on high, she thought, yet this breeze is not blowing anywhere else around the room, only on the mother and baby. She couldn't take anymore, she wanted to scream her lungs out. Then the matron walked in.

"What is it, Nurse, are you alright?"

"Yes, Matron," she said, taking control of herself, "everything is okay."

"Why didn't you tell Topsy that Mr and Mrs Wade are here?" said Matron, still a bit suspicious of this young lady who looked faint.

"You tell her, Matron, I can't," the nurse said, walking away with her head down and nearly bumping into the sister who was just coming in.

"What's with her, she alright?" said the sister looking at the door.

"I'm not sure," said Matron, "We'll have to keep an eye on her. I hate telling Topsy this, but it has to be done. You go on back, Sister. Keep an eye on that young nurse, also tell Mr and Mrs Wade that we shouldn't be long," Matron said, making towards the bed. This is going to hurt me as much as you, Topsy, but I am strong enough to disguise my feelings, she thought, as she looked down at mother and baby now both asleep.

"Topsy, Topsy, you awake" she said, as she gently shook her shoulders.

"Eh, what you want, Matron?" said Topsy, picking up the baby.

"I've come to tell you that Mr and Mrs Wade are here, the white family who are going to look after the little one," said Matron, with a sigh of relief. She looked on in shock as Topsy kissed the baby then said, "Go, my little one, fight for the causes you feel are right. Always look for the truth. People today, both black and white, are forgetting about the truth; they are too busy chasing their own rainbows." Then she passed the baby to her. "Here, Matron, take him."

"Eh . . . ? Oh, yes . . . er . . . you alright, Topsy, I can let you hold him a few more minutes more if you want," said Matron, getting a hold of herself.

"No, Matron, you better take fair one now, I still got my little black one. Fair one will be living white but deep in his heart he will always be black."

Matron had hold of the little one, but she was immobilised, not knowing whether to stay or go.

Topsy made her mind up for her, as she said. "Take him now, for my spirit goes with him, he'll never be alone"

The matron spun around, making for the door. As the older woman went out, Topsy said in a whisper, "Goodbye, my little fair one." She burst into tears, feeling her heart break into a million pieces.

Mr and Mrs Wade were in the waiting room as the matron walked in with the baby. They both got up as she handed the baby to Mary Wade.

"Oh, Ted, isn't he an angel?" said Mary, looking lovingly at the baby.

"Yes, dear, he's beautiful," said Ted, touching him rather gingerly.

"How is the mother?" asked Mary, "Should we go and see her before we go?"

"I don't think that would be wise; that woman I took the baby from doesn't seem to be the same Topsy. Parting with the baby has really shattered her," said Matron.

"What can we do to help?" said Mary, feeling sorry for her, "Give her money?"

"Money won't buy back her baby but, can I give you some advice?" said Matron, trying to sort out her own emotions.

"Yes, please do," said Ted.

"Please sit down, both of you," she said, because she also wanted to sit down. I am mentally exhausted, she thought.

Ted and Mary sat down, whilst the matron pulled up a chair in front of them, so that she could speak directly to both of them.

"I have worked in this hospital for four years now as a matron. Hopefully I will be here for another four years. I love this town, although I was born and bred in the city. We have a lot of Aboriginal people coming and going from this hospital. I am not going into any details, but I feel it very important that my staff learn as much as possible about their customs, and we are still learning about their ways. We have not even scratched the surface yet. They have been here since the beginning of time," she said, "How do we know that they weren't there looking at Eve take a bite of that apple, which brought us all undone?"

"We, the white race, have only been here for two hundred years. We have forced our lifestyle upon these people; the ones that rebelled, we shot, plain and simple. The point I want to stress is this – don't take his Aboriginality away from him, encourage him to pursue the Dreamtime and, above all, let him be proud of his race."

"Thank you, Matron, for what you have told us. I'm sure Ted and I will do our utmost to see that he achieves his goals. Won't we, Ted?" said Mary, looking at her husband.

"Of couse, dear," said Ted. "I, for one, and probably Tommy also, will be going camping in the bush on weekends."

"Suggest it to him, if you get any response, go for it," said Matron, beginning to laugh.

"Let's say we let him grow up first," said Mary, also laughing.

"Absolutely!" said Ted, "one day at a time."

"How old is Tommy?" asked Matron, remembering that they already had a child.

"He's eight," said Ted, "but don't worry, he is all excited about his new baby brother. He's waiting in Perth with my sister."

"Yes, Ted, I can just see all the emotional joy, when we get back," said Mary, thanking God for this little bundle of life.

"You know you'll get a lot of friction amongst your own people?" Matron said.

"Yes, Matron," said Ted, "We understand that the issue will always crop up."

"Let's cross those bridges when we come to them," said Mary, "I want to be part of his learning."

"Yes, of course. Have you thought of a name for him yet?" said Matron.

"No, but I think Ted has something," said Mary.

"Not exactly, anyway, I'd rather the whole family were together," said Ted.

"Yes, by all means," said Matron.

"Well," said Matron, getting up, "I suppose I'd better let you two go — or three, I should say. I guess you've got a lot of talking to do," she said, adjusting the blanket on baby.

"Yes, we do appreciate the advice you've given us," said Ted, putting his arm around his wife's shoulder.

"Okay, then, you've got the letter from the doctor, his record of birth, no complications all in all" said Matron, giving Mary a hug.

"Thank you again, you've been wonderful," said Mary as she and Ted waved goodbye to her.

Walking back along the corridor to see Topsy, Matron had time to reflect on the last few hours. As she checked her patients, she kept wondering, Is it right or wrong for the elderly gentlemen to make laws. Their women have no say in their tribal decisions apart from having babies, gathering food and looking after the little ones. What are they? A shadow for their menfolk to vent their anger, their frustrations, their sexual needs. I can't understand the women; they seem happy playing the secondary role. If a European woman was subjected to that lifestyle, all hell would break loose. Matron shook her head and stepped into Topsy's ward. My, what a different picture now. There was Topsy sitting up in bed playing with the little dark one.

"Hello, Topsy," she said in a soft voice.

"Hello, Matron," Topsy said, not taking her eyes off the baby.

"How are you feeling now?" said Matron, looking closely at Topsy.

"Good. I don't feel so bad inside me now. I

think my ancestors say, 'Topsy, be good now, look after little one for he will be made a special spear and it will hit the kangaroo right in the heart'."

"Can I have a hold of him?" said Matron, with her arms out.

"Here," said Topsy, giving her the baby.

"My, isn't he gorgeous?" said Matron, as she cuddled him, "Look, Topsy, don't blame yourself for one mistake or are you not supposed to?"

"Not one, Matron, but three: getting drunk, having a man, then having two babies."

"But that's ridiculous!" said Matron, pulling up a chair and sitting down with the baby. May as well keep her talking before she clams up on me, thought Matron.

"Topsy, you live so far out in the bush, it was a natural thing to do when you came into town."

"Might be for you, Matron, but not for me."

"That's not what I mean," said Matron, "Look, I'll tell you how I met my husband. I went out with some friends to this hotel in Perth; this is going back a bit. Anyway, my two girlfriends had their boyfriends so I was left at the table, watching them dancing. Then along came the best looking young man there. He asked me for a dance and we've been together ever since. You do understand what I'm trying to say, Topsy?"

"Yes, Matron, I do, but you don't," said Topsy, as she got the baby back from Matron.

"What do you mean?" asked Matron, thinking Topsy's mind was like a deep cave filled up with so many secrets. Let her give me one, thought

Matron.

"Here, Matron, take little one back to his cot, I'm feeling sleepy now," said Topsy, giving Matron the baby.

"Okay, then," said Matron, taking the baby. "You get some rest now."

As Matron took the little one to his cot, she knew that Topsy was feigning sleepiness, but she wasn't about to push her for answers. Given time alone, she may tell me. In the meantime, I'll go on looking after these people whenever they come into my hospital, she thought.

When Topsy knew that the matron had gone, she lay back and thought of the tribal laws she had broken. Will I get a spear pushed through my thigh, or some other punishment they think appropriate? Whatever decision the elders came to, she would willingly accept, but the thought of being banished from the tribe sent shivers down her spine. Anything else but that, I would rather grab a spear and push it deep into my heart and let my blood seep into the soil. She knew it would break fair one's heart if she did, but if she had to choose between banishment and death, she would choose death because banishment was death itself.

She had made three mistakes. The first was getting drunk, for she knew the elders disapproved of any form of alcohol.

Why, why did I go into town? I should have said no, her mind screamed at her.

Her second mistake was getting involved with

that white man. She was too drunk to remember anything of that night, but how could she tell the elders that. They would not understand. The worst part of this nightmare was that she was a give-away. When she was a baby, she was given to a young boy of a neighbouring tribe. He and the other young men of the tribe were out in the desert going through the initiation ceremonies helped by a couple of the elders. They would not be back for six months or more.

The third mistake was to have two babies. It had been passed down through tribal law going back over many rains upon rains that each women in the tribe was allowed only one baby. If she had two, death would claim one, either taken care of by the elders or nature itself. That is why she had to get rid of fair one. Yes, she had made her ancestors' spirits angry, because carrying two babies would be too much for her on walkabout and, with two mouths to feed, she would have to gather twice as much food as the other women.

In time, little fair one will grow up to be strong and healthy and my spirit will always be calling him back to the red brown soil wherever he goes. But I will not let them banish me, fair one. I will kill myself before banishment. You will know by the wise old owl.

She turned over on her side. She was getting tired, sleep was slowly covering her as she closed her eyes and said, "Mummy loves you, little fair one."

Eighteen

Singer Songwriter

Jim was backstage, picking out a few notes on his guitar. Nothing in particular, just strumming, trying to combat his nervousness, for he was to go on next, after the Nyoongar band already on stage. This was his first public appearance. The audience consisted mainly of Nyoongars who were highly charged. There were also a few watjellas. Oh, God, Jim thought, I wonder how they will take me? I'm only a bush Nyoongar, not terribly sought after. I can do it! I can do it! I can do it! He got those four little words going repeatedly through his mind.

"Hello, brother," said a member of a Nyoongar rock band who was waiting to go on tonight. There were also a few solo artists and Jim was one of them. "Here, have a charge," said the bloke, passing a bottle of whisky towards him, "this will calm you down, you will feel good. The beat will come from your heart."

"No, thanks, koordah," said Jim.

"Wanna puff then?" said the bloke, "Just as good, if not better. Put them together and you come up with words and beautiful music, a singer songwriter, man."

"Look, koordah, I'm just fine," said Jim, feeling annoyed with the bloke.

"Okay, koordah, I get the message," said the bloke, "sit there and shit yourself. I know when I first went on about two years ago, I was so charged up with gunja and gerbah, music just came naturally, freely, flowing from my body." The bloke paused, then added, "Now every time we do a gig, I gotta be high. I just can't go out there if I'm not spaced out."

"You're joking, man," said Jim, then realised this guy was for real.

"I wish I was," said the bloke. "You see, it gives me confidence in womankind. I know I've got a problem, but man, the way I feel now, it's a beautiful problem." Laughing his head off, he walked away from Jim, full of confidence.

Jim was left there on his own, strumming and wondering whether he had done the right thing or not. His brains were having a game of tug-of-war with him. One half was screaming, "You should have taken it, for it would've settled you down, make the audience respond to you, and you likewise to them." The other half of his brain was saying, "No, no, you don't need that shit to prove how good you are. Only you know that, go out with a clear mind and put your body and spirit into what you love doing best, that's singing."

Jim's mind wandered back to when he was a boy growing up in a little wheat belt town about four hours drive from Perth. They were fun days, although his parents scrimped from day to day, he always felt love in the blackfella community. They were always sharing, helping each other out with tucker, or whatever. He could still hear his mother saying to him, "Now, Jimmy, go and ask Aunty so and so for tea, milk, flour, sugar or butter." And whatever family had the goods, always gave, just like his mother did. Whatever kids came over asking for things, Mum, without hesitation, gave. If she had a bit extra, she would put it aside for whoever came next to ask for something,

Tears welled up in Jim's eyes as he thought of his mother, God rest her soul. Swallowing a lump in his throat, he thought, I wish Mum was here to see me on stage, for she would be my number one fan. I reckon God would be getting her to make those big beautiful dampers up there somewhere. Yes, I'd say God would make her the number one cook.

Jim had seen his father, a strong hard-working man, wilt before his very eyes like leaves on a tree in autumn, falling slowly from a branch to the ground, waiting for the wind to whisk them away into eternity. A victim of alcoholic onslaught. His uncles, his aunties, and cousins were also caught up in this vicious web. They were like insects, trying to break free. If they did, a bigger, stronger web awaited them, for they seemed doomed forever in an alcoholic tomb. Why is my race, the Nyoongar people, a sitting duck to drugs and alcohol? Is it an escape route from reality? Or, like the bloke said, "It gives me confidence."

"Hey, come on, man," Jim said to himself. "Concentrate on what you are about to do." The backstage was getting a bit crowded as members of different groups wandered in and out checking to see when they were going on.

"Hey, Jim, you know you got an hour to go." It was Tommy, his mate, coming towards him.

"What? I thought I was on next," said Jim, feeling as though one of his guitar strings had just broken in the middle of a song.

"Now, now, settle down, koordah, the organisers have just told me," said Tommy, calming him down.

"That's all I need, koordah," said Jim, looking around him. "Yeah, apparently they want this other band on, it's pretty popular, but don't worry, Jim, you'll get your chance," said Tommy, hoping he'd see reason.

"By the time I get out there, they'll be bombed out of their brains. They wouldn't know if I was singing *Onward Christian Soldiers* or John Lennon's, *Imagine*," said Jim, totally pissed off.

"Look, koordah, next week your tapes will be on the market. These people here are like anyone else, they like to see the artist before they buy," said Tommy. "When they see and hear you sing, they'll be getting John Lennon, Elvis, Billy Joel and Bruce Springsteen all rolled into one," giving him that extra push, "plus you'll be on the airwaves on Friday, you'll be getting a lot of exposure within the next two to three weeks."

"Yeah, but . . . "

"No buts, koordah," said Tommy, cutting him off, trying to get him in the right frame of mind.

Tommy, like a brother to Jim, was brought up in the same wheat belt town. Tommy was a few years older, more or less a manager type and Jim always sought and respected his advice.

"No wonder half of these guys here are freaking out. Typical Nyoongars, they give you a time to perform and it's not the right time. Why don't they give you a time to start on and forget the rest of the time," said Jim, "How long to go?"

"Not long," said Tommy looking at his watch.

"Here, hang on to my guitar," said Jim passing the faithful instrument to Tommy, "Headin' for a piss."

Jim had to walk past the bar. The band was really belting out the notes. The audience was running on high, some dancing, a few at the bar, others stamping their feet and swaying to the beat of the music. All in all, they looked a pretty orderly mob. This band playing now was from Queensland. Their music consisted of Thursday Island, Palm Island and Aboriginal. Put together, they sounded like reggae, rock, blues and soul, all blending beautifully.

Jim entered the toilets. Christ, he thought, even in here they're passing the bottle and gunja around, the bloody drug squad would have a ball in here. The aroma just lingered in the air. Jim stepped back, zipped himself up, washed his hands, dried them and looked up to see a big blackfella looking down at him. Oh, God, no, thought Jim, don't tell me this big bastard wants to punch my lights out. He stood frozen.

"How are you going, koordah?" said the big fella, extending his hand out, "My name's Shorty."

"Not too bad, koordah, Jim's the name," he grabbed the big fella's hand, shaking it. "I see why they call you Shorty," he said for this fella was well over six foot, pretty close to seven.

"Yeah," he laughed, "My uncle call me that. He reckon I grow too fast, more quicker than a mulga tree."

"Where about you come from?" said Jim looking at his cowboy clothes and riding boots. Must be from north, he also speaks good English, which probably is his second language, thought Jim.

"Other side of Wiluna, not far from the NT border," said Shorty, showing off his pearly white teeth.

"You grow 'em any taller up that way?" asked Jim, who, at five foot ten and a half (in the old yards, feet, and inches), was practically looking at Shorty's chest.

"They more higher than me further up," he laughed, "and more blacker." By this time there were a few more Nyoongars gathered around the conversation and they all burst out laughing.

"Shit," said one Nyoongar, "You'd make a solid ruckman."

"Yeah," another bloke asked, "You ever played footy?"

Shorty looked at him a little confused.

"You know, footy," he said, doing the actions.

He looked more like a ballet dancer than a footballer going through the motions. Shorty wasn't registering at all, so the ballet dancer grabbed the bottle rather quickly from his mate, and passed it to Shorty, hoping Shorty would realise that he wasn't trying to make a clown out of him.

"Here, koordah, have a charge," begged the ballet dancer.

"No, I don't drink," Shorty told him. "My tribe say no good, so I listen to my elders."

Christ, that's a turn up, thought Jim. It's a pity these Nyoongars here in Perth couldn't take a leaf from their book.

"How long you down for?" asked Jim.

"Not too long, maybe next week I go back," he responded.

"You cruel big bloke," said the ballet dancer's mate.

"Yeah, boy, if you were my brother, I'd pick all the fights out with these watjellas and some of these good-for-nothing Nyoongars here," said ballet dancer.

"'Course, we'd make 'em piss," exclaimed his mate, throwing a couple of left jabs.

"Let's get outta here," said Jim, "Shorty, can I

talk to you outside?"

"Yeah, koordah," said Shorty, as he and Jim made for the door. It was getting crowded in there and Shorty was taking up all the space.

The noise from the band was deafening. The drummer was trying to smash the drums to smithereens with those two small sticks. The crowd was really in the groove, the bar, as usual, was quite popular.

"Come back stage, Shorty" said Jim, beckoning Shorty to follow, "It's a bit quieter there."

As they went back stage, Tommy and a few blokes who were there, gasped at this big blackfella following Jim.

Hell, he must be seven foot tall, thought Tommy. Where did Jim find him?

"Tommy, meet a friend I've just met," said Jim, grabbing the guitar from Tommy. "This is Shorty, and this is Tommy," said Jim introducing them, with a smile on his face. Tommy was shorter than Jim so it was funny watching him shaking hands with Shorty.

"Let's sit down," suggested Tommy, becoming aware of the sight they created. Tommy, himself, chuckled, thinking about it. "How long now?" asked Jim, bringing the chairs over.

"About fifteen minutes," responded Tommy.

"You playing here directly?" asked Shorty, setting himself down.

"Yeah, going on next. If everything goes to plan," remarked Jim, looking at Tommy.

"No worries, koordah, you most definitely be

on next. These guys are flying back to Brisbane just before midnight, so they'll be cutting it fine getting to the airport," said Tommy.

"Can you play a tune for me?" asked Shorty.

"All depends on what you want," said Jim, knowing full well, it had to be a Slim Dusty song.

"You play me a Slim Dusty. When I go back to my country, I will tell my tribe a big star sing for me and our people," he smiled.

"What song do you want, Shorty?" hoping for an easy one because he wasn't too familiar with Slim, not like his father and uncles. Some weekends, when they were drinking, it turned into a Slim Dusty marathon.

"*Min Min Light*," said Shorty smiling.

"Oh, shit, I don't know that one," said Jim, "How about *The Pub With No Beer*?" Strumming and singing quietly, he stopped and said to Shorty, "Tell me about your tribe and how do they live, you said no alcohol allowed out there."

"No," said Shorty, looking around back stage. It seemed an entirely different world for him.

"No grog allowed. You see, five elders, my father and his four brothers, they run a . . . how would you say . . . a community up there. There are six families all living together; no arguments, men go for kangaroos, emus and bungarras, while women go for bardies, flour from the seeds of the land, dig for rabbits and sometimes they get goannas. We gottem four-wheel drive, rifles, dogs, axe and shovels, plenty water there, old people know where gold is. This why they sent me to Perth to take another four-wheel drive back."

"What . . . gold?" asked Tommy, ears pricking up on hearing that irresistible word.

Shorty laughed, "We don't know, only my two old uncles know. Whenever we want something, five old mans sit down and talk about it. Then they go away at night, then they take me into Wiluna buy clothes for me, give me money for four-wheel drive. When I get back to Wiluna, I take my clothes off, give to my cousin and drive back to my country."

"What happens when some one breaks the law? You know, like fight or being drunk or even belting his wife up?" asked Jim, really getting interested.

"No chance for drink, Wiluna four hundred k's away. When some one break community law, whether man or woman, elders send them to desert, maybe two or one week, on their own."

"What about the kids?" asked Tommy, who couldn't believe this life existed, in this day and age.

"Boys and girls from twelve upwards, if caught petrol sniffing or stealing or giving cheek to the elders, were sent to the desert on their own. But always with an elder within visual distance. But they don't know."

"How do they survive?" asked Jim, who also couldn't get over it.

"From the land. They are given a spear, then told to go. Maybe for two or three days depending on how bad the crime is," said Shorty, realising these Nyoongar people knew nothing of his life style. To us, he thought, it's like the hot sun on the sand or the cold night wind that comes off the desert.

"Hey Jimbo, you're on pretty soon," a stage hand called out.

"Hell, I can talk to you all night and all day tomorrow," said Jim getting up and getting his guitar.

"Yeah, it's a real eye opener," said Tommy, "You alright then, Jim?"

"Look, Shorty, you go out front, I'll sing your Slim Dusty first and then I'll sing my two, right," said Jim.

"It was good to meet you, koordah," said Shorty. "Also you, too," shaking Tommy's hands.

"You listen to the words of the last song, Shorty. You see, I wrote it, I think about three weeks ago and I think the spirits of your ancestors sent you down here to hear this song. It's about your life up in your country. What we Nyoongars are searching for. Our spirits are forming a bond with your spirits," said Jim, feeling that he wasn't knotted up any more as he watched the big black giant make his way out to the front. Jim couldn't get over the feeling, his mother's spirit was around somewhere close. It wasn't a coincidence, as Jim whispered, "I love you, Mum, may your spirit stay over me, protect me from all wrong doings."

"I can't believe it," whispered Tommy, "that song you wrote three weeks ago was intended for

Shorty and his tribe, but you met him tonight for the first time. Is it fate or what? Coincidence or whatever they call it?"

"Trouble with you, koordah," said Jim, putting an arm around his shoulder "you let your mind be dominated by yorgahs, gerbah, gunja and wondering where our next dollar coin is coming from, keep you mind open."

"What else is there to worry about? You gone religious or something?" asked Tommy, looking at Jim to see if he's okay. "Where's that uptight singer songwriter who was here an hour ago, anyway?" enquired Tommy, becoming aware of Jim's more relaxed feeling.

"He has flown the coop" said Jim, as heard his name being called out.

"Now, ladies and gentlemen, we have a Nyoongar making his first appearance tonight. Singer Songwriter, Jimbo Naltjie . . . a big hand please."

"Make 'em piss" said Tommy, patting him on the back.

Everyone was clapping as he came to the mike. Some were shouting, some whistling, in all they were running on high. They are really into it, he thought, shielding his eyes from the glare of the light shining onto the stage. Impossible to see Shorty. Then the big blackfella stood up. Christ, you could see him a hundred miles away, he thought, as he waved to Shorty. His backing group was ready. They didn't like a Slim Dusty song to kick off with, but Tommy and Jim had talked them into it.

"Thank you, ladies and gentlemen, I'm going to start off with Slim Dusty's hit, called *The Pub with No Beer*."

He heard groans of "Oh, no," from the crowd and then Shorty's great booming voice coming over the top, "Good on ya, koordah."

He let it rip. "It's a lonesome away . . . "

It surprised him that the audience were all singing along with him. Shit, he thought, as he sang, the old people brought these kids up right. By the time he finished, anyone would think this song was number one in the top ten today, the way it was easily sung by the crowd. It sure was a good old song. His next was a song, Stand By Me and was sung by John Lennon. He knew he had the audience in his hand. He could feel them warming right up to him.

Tommy watched from the wings, he couldn't believe his eyes for out there performing was a seasoned campaigner, not a first timer. How does he do it? he thought.

When that was over, he had them screaming for more. Jim was feeling at ease, wiping the perspiration from his brow. He looked across at Tommy, who was standing there at the wings, still clapping and giving him the thumbs up sign. Shit, he thought, if Tommy can give me the all clear sign, I must be doing well. The crowd was still clapping, but as Jim held up his hands in the air, the clapping ceased.

"Now ladies and gentlemen, this next song I'm

about to sing is about our Aboriginal people. We can all relate to this song which was written by me, and I'd like to dedicate this song to a friend I met tonight. To Shorty and his tribe, for he will understand the words. If you all listen to the words, it has some wonderful meaning."

The haunting sound of the didgeridoo started, then the band joined in the haunting melody. As Jim prepared himself for the song he loved, he could feel his mother's presence along with all his ancestors spirits. I'm sure they are harmonising with me, he thought as he started to sing. The words went like this:

I got no money in my pocket
Just a guitar in my hand
So come on my dark skin beauty
Let's go back to our tribal land.

We had enough of the city.
I feel the spirits are calling me,
Back to the red-brown country.
Where our bodies are free.

Sittin' by a camp fire
Lookin' up at the stars.
Oh, I do feel at peace,
Knowing just where we are.

I don't care for the money
Only the guitar in my hand.

I'm back where I came from
In my tribal land.

The crowd screamed for more as he finished off that haunting song. Everyone wanted more as he raised his hands to silence the crowd. "Thank you, ladies and gentlemen, I'm afraid that's all the time which is allowed to me. But I'd like to say to Shorty, your country is our country and our country is your country. Thank you all and may the spirits of your ancestors, watch and protect you. And may God bless you all."

As he made for the wings, he could still hear the crowd screaming, "We want Jimbo! We want Jimbo! We want Jimbo!" Smiling in front of him was Tommy, who grabbed and hugged him saying, "You made 'em piss, brotherrr."

Nineteen

Long Time Now

"Teddy, what for you being slow, hurry an' go to school," shouted his mother in an angry voice. He got up from his chair rather nonchalantly and stood by the fire, his eye's glued to the television set.

"Hurry up dis minute, you might be a tall fifteen year old, but you not too big to hit," she screamed, turning the television off. "Hab a shower and put some clean clothes on, g'orn, get."

Teddy made his way to his wardrobe, grabbed some clothes and headed for the shower. Under the warm water, he felt good. He thought about his life. Since his father died three years ago of a drug overdose, his own life was the pits. He loved his English classes and especially his English teacher, Miss what's-her-name, Maria somebody.

She wore her mini-skirt up as far as they were allowed to go, and man, when she bent over, it just about blew you away. She'd have to be Spanish, with those big brown eyes, her beautiful black shoulder-length hair that makes a bloke's tongue touch the ground.

"Hey, Teddy, me boy," he said out loud, "you're getting yourself excited just thinking about her." Anyway, he thought, she'd have to be around twenty seven or eight, much too old for you. Think about home, this will stop your excitement. He thought how everything turned upside down since Dad had died.

His father was a watjella and his mother was a Nyoongar, quite dark. He didn't care what colour her skin was though, he loved her. Ted has a thirteen year old sister who, he thinks, is fuckin' crazy. She was on dope but not the hard stuff that Dad had overdosed on. Every time she'd come home, he'd get her away from Mother and lift her sleeves up and check her arm very closely. He would say to her,

"If I catch you messin' around with Harry or any of that heavy shit, I'll kill you before the needle does."

His dad was an A1 plus in his eyes, but, fuckin' Harry had to fuck his life up; not only his, but ours, too, he thought. Aloud, he said, "Holy shit! It's Saturday today. Mum's got me like a zombie. Whatever she says, I do." I think I'll write a book on my life, he thought.

"Hey, Mum," he shouted. Better turn the shower down. "Hey, Mum," much louder. He heard her footsteps at the door. "Mum," he shouted again.

"What you want?" came her reply.

"It's Saturday and there is no school 'til Tuesday, seeing it's a long weekend."

"Unna," he heard her say, then heard her footsteps go away,

Adjusting the shower back to the right temperature, he felt the warmth spread all over his body. I could stay under here all morning, he thought, I wonder if Jillie's home. Should've asked Mum. I'm sure, yes, I am sure she is. She was in bed when I got home. God, wish I could spend the night with Miss Marie somebody, my pretty senorita. I will be your knight in shining armour. I will ride across the green fields with the reins in my left hand, with a pretty rose clenched between my teeth and I will scoop you up in my right arm and ride into the forest with you. "Fuck off, Ted, you're a dreamer, man," he said to himself.

There was a banging on the door and Jill was practically screaming. "Get out of this shower, Teddy, I want to go to the toilet."

Hell, he thought, one minute I was riding through the forest with my pretty senorita and the next I'm back where I started from.

"Come on, Teddy, I wanna go to the toilet . . . please," Jill almost begged.

Slipping on his jeans and shirt to open the door to his little sister, she dashed towards the toilet, pushing him out of the way, saying, "G'orn, fuck off outta here."

"Yeah, 'good morning' to you, too," he said closing the door.

Jillie's in a shitty mood, he thought. When she starts swearing so early in the morning, it's gonna be a bad day.

Walking towards his mother, he grabbed her and gave her a great big hug, then releasing her, he said in the best manly voice he could muster.

"Mum, I'm going on for sixteen and I would appreciate it if you and Jilly could call me Ted. Look I'm almost a grown man," he almost begged, towering over her.

"You still my little boy to me," making a playful swipe at him with the tea towel

I give in, he thought. "Yeah, thanks, Mum, I'll have what ever you got"

"Dus good," she said.

You could put Mum in the highest university in the world and she'd confuse the greatest academics in the literature field with her Nyoongar slang, he thought, smiling to himself.

"What you bin smilin' for," she asked, "some yorgah, I bettem you."

"No, Mum, I'm happy that you've cooked this beautiful breakfast for me."

"I know you like your eggs an' toast," she said, beaming at the young man before her. Who woulda thought he turn out dis way. Little skinny runt, now almos' six foot, more I think. Sitting across from him and sipping her tea, she thought, proper like 'im father, same eyes, same colour hair an' so good lookin', no wonder da yorgah's come here alla time. He know I loved his father, but dose drugs no good. His father was a watjella an' um a Nyoongar but dat didn't stop our love. The hurt in her eyes showed and he noticed straight away and asked "You alright, Mother?"

"Course um orright," she said.

He knew she was hurting and the pain she went through. He couldn't blame her for hurting and he gave her a hug and held her to him, giving her a big kiss on the cheek and saying with his heart, "I really love you, Mum".

"Yeah, you good boy, Teddy, but don't touch dose drugs. You know I hate em, an' look what dey done to your father," she said with a hurtful expression.

Holding her tight, he tried to gauge her hurt. He spoke to her in a loving way. "Mother, I know it's over three years now since that fateful night father died. I know you are hurting for him and you'll never forget him, Mum," he said softly, almost a whisper. "You know I love and miss him too; so does Jilly. I often catch her cryin', holding onto a photo of Dad. I've joined her in crying for Dad, but we have got to come to terms with it."

"Is Jilly takin' dem drugs and why she shout an swear for alla time," she questioned him.

"Let's go to the lounge and sit down. I'll make you a cup of tea and we'll have a talk," he said as he guided her into the lounge, settled her down on her favorite seat and pulled the curtains, letting in the beautiful sunshine which filled the room with light.

Making his mother a cup of tea, he thought of ways of telling her about Jill. He didn't want to tell her a bare-faced lie, nor did he want Jilly to feel aggressive towards him by his dobbing her in to Mum. In actual fact, Jilly looked up to him for encouragement and support and he thought it would be injudicious to let on all to Mum. Maybe, just maybe, he thought, I'll tell Mum what she wants to hear and I'll keep the real information of her taking gunja to myself. He was so exasperated that he thought his brain was going to explode. His mother was a gentle woman, absorbing all her hurt and pain and not once, he thought, did she show her hurt openly towards me and Jilly. She did show some hurt at the funeral, but I was supporting her and Jilly. I had to be strong. There were so many people there, watjellas and Nyoongars. It was quite traumatic and confusing for a thirteen year old boy to see his Dad's coffin lowered into the ground.

"Hey, Teddy boy, what you bin doin', you makin' 'em tea or what," she called out from the lounge.

"Yeah, Mum, just gettin' myself a drink of orange juice," he called back to his mum. Wow, he thought, I think I completly lost it for awhile there, shaking his head. Passing his mother a cup of tea, he touched his glass of orange juice to her cup and said, "Cheers, Mum."

She sipped her tea with a look of calm and tranquillity about her. Ted didn't want to push or force her into a conversation. If she wanted to, she'll talk, if not, no big deal.

Sipping her tea, his mother looked at Ted and smiled and said. "Your father was good to me, he always cared," then falling back into her Nyoongar slang subconciously, with a knowing look in her eyes that shone with adoration and love, she said, "I 'member when I was a young gal at school. Maybe thirteen, maybe fourteen. Well, your father 'im be-e-e say fifteen or sixteen, nearly same as you, real good lookin', too. He coulda hab any watjella yorgah he wanted an' dere was lotta purty one's dere. He reckon to me I was da purtiest one dere," she said, blushing. "Choo, um gettin' shame now," she said, giggling.

"No, no, Mum, go on," he said eagerly. "You used to tell me and Jilly all the time. But we were too young to remember then. I know Jilly was too young, but I can remember a lot you told me. Tell me about your father," he asked.

"Your grandfather, Teddy, dus where you got your name from. Watjella bin gib him dat, cause dey couldn't say his gibben Aboriginal name, so dey called him Edward Jackie Singer, Ted for short," she smiled at her young son. He could see by the glow in her eyes that she was communicating with the past, going back in time. The excitement and intensity was flowing out of the pores of her skin like water that refreshes the dry soil. A tiny trickle of a tear softly made its way to her mouth and as she tasted it, she saw the figure of her father so visibly in her mind.

"Mum, you alright," asked Ted with concern,

"if it's hurting you, you don't have to talk about the past."

"But I want to, my boy," she said, with an excited air. The freedom and the acknowledgement of turning on the tap and letting the history of her people run free from her soul, was comforting, somehow. It whetted the appetite of her young son, whose eagerness to learn his family history was quite extraordinary in itself. Added to this was the determination on her part to tell her son as much as she could of his grandfather and great grandfather. Her father had told her stories before she was taken by the Native Protectors or Native Welfare and these she now passed on to her son.

*

"Your great grandfather, my grandfather, hadda Aboriginal name like da wise ol' owl an' he knew when to go an' when to stop. He something like a medicine man. Choo, he like he was 'ere one minute an' den he gone da next. Dey say he was like a spirit, but I bin seen 'im, when I little," she said, looking at her young son's face. His expression, showing the anticipation and the eagerness so like his great grandfather, was overwhelming. As this was the first time she had actually spoken of her grandfather, she was pleased that it was to her own son and in her Nyoongar language. Or as young Teddy would say, "in her Nyoongar slang."

She told him about the time she and her mother were walking to the river to get some water. Her mother was a young woman then and she was a little girl. Her mother was walking ahead of her while she was running among the wildflowers, smelling some and picking some for her mother, who would often stop and call in her Nyoongar tongue, "If you don't hurry up, a bad spirit is going to grab you and take you away. No more little Nora."

In response, Nora would run as fast as her little legs would carry her, not letting go of the wildflowers, which she tightly clung to. At the same time, she had to duck the magpies, which swooped down at her head for daring to come too close to their nest that held their young. Her mother would laugh at her as she watched her little girl run to her, bobbing and weaving through the grass and wild flowers, shrieking for her to help her. But her mother wanted to teach her a lesson; that the magpie had as much right to the woods as she did. The magpie chased anything that was moving or intruded on their domain.

Finally, running to her mother who scooped her up in her arms, she nestled herself into her mother's bosom, slyly peeking out for the magpie, which was not in sight. Finding courage, she tilted her head back and looked directly into her mother's face. Her mother was laughing beyond control, which got little Nora into a laughing frenzy too. Pulling the bunch of wildflowers, which she still had clasped in her mother's bosom, she slowly withdrew the flowers and offered them to her mother, who had managed to control herself and gave Nora a loving hug and said to her in her Nyoongar tongue, "Although that Magpie was chasin' you, not once did you drop those flowers to protect your head with your hands. Your only thought was for me, your mother. May the spirits of our ancestors watch over you and keep you, to obey the laws of the land, trees, waters and rocks.

Then she heard a booming laugh within the trees and she wondered who it was. Her mother whispered in her ear excitedly and said, "It's my father, your grandfather," in her Nyoongar tongue. He walked from the shadows of the trees and embraced his daughter and grabbing his little granddaughter, he threw her into the air and caught her as if she was a small pebble. Delight took over from fear and little Nora wanted him to throw her as high as he could. She wanted to touch the moon, the stars and to play amongst the clouds, while her mother looked at her daughter and father in adoration.

Passing Nora to her mother, they walked to the shade of a tree. He spoke to her in earnestness, telling her to be wary and not walk around by herself and his granddaughter alone in the woods. There were a lot of watjellas going around the bush with their black trackers. Harm could come to her and little Nora.

He spoke very fluently in his tongue and his words were quite rapid and she picked up on the occasional word and managed to get a bleak picture of what was in store for them. Before he disappeared, he told his daughter with great concern, in his Nyoongar tongue, "Be very careful of the white man from across the sea. He has banded together a group of black trackers and the white man has installed all his hate into the black soldiers' hearts making them the most feared amongst our Nyoongar people. They are merely puppies on a chain, but let loose, they become ferocious dogs. They will attack mainly women and children. The white man has taught them well to maim and destroy their own people, along with these white people who carry the Bible. I must go now," he whispered in his Nyoongar tongue.

He gave her mother a hug that little Nora thought was going to last forever. She clung to her mother's leg in silent tears. Bending to pick little Nora up, he held her to his chest and kissing away her tears, he said, "Look after your mother and beware of the dark shadows, for you know not what lurks within them."

Putting her down, he indicated with his lips, eyes and head that he had to go. Not a word was spoken. At that precise moment, as if by magic, a strong willy willy danced and twirled around mother and daughter. Her mother grabbed little Nora and shielded her from the wind, buried her face into her bosom. It was a matter of seconds before calmness crept back to the woods and everything was still, even the leaves on the trees breathed a sigh of relief. She managed to disengage herself from her mother and quickly looked around for her grandfather, who was nowhere to be seen.

With questions and tears in her eye's, she looked at her Mother for answers. None was forthcoming. As her mother held her and brushed the tears from her eyes, she said quietly "Come, my little wildflower, get some water and come quickly. Your father is waiting for us."

"Teddy, you orright, you look like you not here in dis house," she asked, snapping him back to reality.

"Uh . . . yeah, Mum. No, that was awesome, fascinating, astonishing, incredible or just plain 'wow'. You, your mother, father and grandfather. But where was your grandmother?" he asked.

With eyes downcast, she told him what the black trackers did to her grandmother. While her father and grandfather went hunting, these black trackers and white troopers came upon their camp. Her grandmother was left behind to look after the place. The black trackers, with encouragement from the white troopers, proceeded to brutalize her and burn their camp down. The white troopers also participated in the carnal destruction of the camp and the frail Nyoongar woman.

"Did they find her body"? Ted asked, seething with anger. "Yeah, but she was not a purty sight," she said, letting the tears run free. Ted held his mother and comforted her and let her have a good cry.

"Come on, Mum, you lie down and have a good rest. You can tell me more when you feel better." She nodded her head and let him support her to the bedroom. Making sure that she was comfortable, Ted slipped out of the room and sat in the lounge. He let his mind go backward and forward. It was like yesterday, to-day, and tomorrow, zipping back and forth at an incredible speed. I've got to get her to tell me about her father, my grandfather, who must have been an amazing man, he thought.

"Hey, what you sittin' so quiet and crazy-like," called Jill, who was standing at the door.

She had disrupted his train of thought. "Uh . . . hey . . . just got out of bed, have ya."

"Yeah, sort of. I did go back to bed, got up and had a shower. What's for breakfast and where's Mum," she asked.

"First question, help yourself to breakfast, sec ond question, Mum is resting and my question to you is, what took you so long to get up?" he asked.

"My answers, went back to bed, just woke up and had a shower. Cheers," she said and walked into the kitchen.

For a girl who is turning fourteen soon, I can't get over it. I mean, she looks more like seventeen or eighteen. I've seen her when she's got on all that make-up, he thought, and she doen't look too bad.

Indeed she was a very atractive young lady. She had light blond hair, brown eyes and skin that gave her a sun tan all year round which made the other girls, especially the white girls, quite envious. She occasionally dabbled in dope, nothing fantastic and her friends also kept away from the heavier stuff. She even considered giving away dope because she vaguely remembered her father's experiences with drugs. She was still quite young, but old enough to feel and absorb the hurt, pain and loneliness experienced by her mother, Teddy and herself.

She couldn't quite understand Teddy. Her brother wanted to take on being the father figure and for most of the time, he'd play the lead role as head of the house. But there were times when he would cry along with her for their father. It was at those time that Teddy wasn't play acting. He was just a small, hurt son crying out for the father he had lost. But sometimes, he would show her the biggest insult and that would be after she'd come home from a fabulous party. He would take her aside, lift the sleeves of her dress up and check to see if there were any puncture wounds on her arms. This would become too infuriating and she let him know by saying, "Piss off, that's not my scene."

Yeah, she thought, just leave all that heavy shit alone. She started thinking of her forty five year old father, who they said, had commited suicide. As the coroner had officially told them, it was death by misadventure. He had put too much heroin into his veins; not calculating the risk he was taking. She loved her father and would never forget him. But each day she had grown stronger and stronger and often said to her mother, "Mum, life must go on, regardless of the circumstances, it was purely unfortunate." Yeah, we are the one's who are suffering, she thought, or should I say, Mum is suffering the most.

Grabbing toast and coffee and making her way to the lounge, where Teddy was still sitting in deep thought, she put down her cup and the plate of toast and began eating, still looking at her brother, who seemed to be in a world of his own.

"What's with you?" she asked between bites of toast.

"Nothing, just sitting here thinking of what Mum told me about her grandfather, our great grandfather and it was 'wow' plus," he said to her, still coming to terms with his powerful anscestors. "But I am hoping that she'll tell us more, no, I mean, I hope Mum can tell me about her father."

"Yeah, I know that, dummie," she responded. "And her father's name was Edward Jackie Singer and that's where you got your name from," she said. Ted scratched his head and was about to ask her a question, when she went on to tell him, "Mum has told me a lot about him, wow, he would have to be the warrior above all warriors."

Sensing that she knew more about their grandfather than he, Ted thought, you could tell Jillie something that happen last year and she'd still remember it, practically word for word. "But, what I mean is, that the way Mum tells the story is, like, you are going way back beyond yesterday and you can actually feel the wind, smell the leaves, hear a babbling brook run it's way to a stream, or even hear the birds singing and flapping their wings as they fly through the air. The look on her face tells you, that you are in the bush, on the same journey as she," he explained.

"You make everything seem so romantic, Teddy. No wonder you are getting top marks in your English classes. Miss Ustazellas must devote more time to you than the other students," she said laughing.

"So that's her last name," he said blushing.

"Of course, Miss Maria Ustazellas. My friends told me that you got the hots for her and, come to think of it, they say that she's got the hots for you," she said, laughing.

This news sent the heat from his face right through his body. I'd better get her off this subject before I start dreaming of her, he thought. "But I want Mum to tell me or both of us together. Of all the shit that he had to go through to protect his daughter, our Mum."

"Yeah, Teddy, I know what you mean. But . . . is Mum up to it?" she asked with a frown on her face.

"That's just it," he said, "She looked pretty well drained after telling me about her grandfather. And I felt that way too."

They spoke of their grandfather, grandmother and, of course, their mother, for whom they had great love and respect. The mission she was brought up in, then her adoption by this watjella family, who looked after her as if she was their own – they discussed all these aspects of their mother's life. The fact that Nora regarded her adoptive parents, who had passed on, as her own, was heart warming.

They also spoke of their own father who had made the unfortunate mistake of overdosing on drugs. He used to dabble in gunja and the story of that fatal night went like this: Their father went for a drink at his mate's place. The usual thing happened, drinking and smoking gunja. The next minute, his mate came to say he was in hospital in a coma. Although it was serious, he was stable, so there was a good chance that he would live. The hospital staff didn't seemed too concerned. This had happend before because of his diabetes, which to all intents and purposes, he had under control. But for a man in his middle forties, one hit of heroin was fatal. According to the coroner's report, he had misjudged his sugar levels with his diabetes and the conclusion was death by misadventure. They talked of how it first upset them and how they were now coming to terms with it. But Mum never spoke of it and didn't show any signs of grieving for her husband, although at times, she did let her defences down and it did show. But she, being a strong Nyoongar woman, dealt with her grief by asking the spirits of her ancestors to guide her through each waking day and to cope with life's difficulties, in giving her a clear head and not to dwell too much in the past.

"What, youse talkin' 'bout me or what?" she asked, startling her two children who looked up at her standing at the door.

"Oh, Mum, you frightened us," called Jilly, holding her chest.

"You okay?" asked Ted. "Jillie, get Mum a cup of tea. I guess you've rested, Mum?" guiding her to a seat and getting her comfortable.

"Course um right, an' how Jilly bin, orright?" she asked

"Yeah, Mum, she's been very good all morning," he told her.

Jill brought the tea in and placed it on the table next to her mother and said, "I believe you've been telling Teddy, here, about our grandfather?"

Nodding her head to Jill and looking at Teddy, she said, "I wanna tell you more. I feel rested now."

"Okay, Mum," responded Ted, trying not to sound too eager. He looked at her eyes and saw the warm glow ignite.

"Yes, your grandfather was a brave Nyoongar warrior." As parts of her childhood, along with that of her father's story began to unfold, she felt better for sharing her story.

*

Her father was captured somewhere around Perth and placed in Moore River Settlement, where he stayed until his teenage years. He didn't know how old he was when he was put in the Settlement but he was very young. He did know his mother, who had been killed by the black trackers. On this particular day, his father had taken him out hunting and when they returned, there was nothing left of the camp.

Eventually, the black trackers caught her father and took him to the settlement. He spent his growing years there. He hated the black trackers. He would spook the black trackers' horses, making them spend all day or most of the day, looking for them. Her father wanted to kill the black trackers as the other Nyoongars looked at them as worthless, no more than white mans' whipping boys. When the black trackers got beaten by their white masters, they would take it out on their own Nyoongar people, men, women and children. The black trackers, were the most feared amongst the Nyoongars. Yarns say that her father had even killed a black tracker with his bare hands, but that was Nyoongars' speculation. Speculation or not, that particular black tracker was never seen again around the settlement or the surrounding area.

The Superintendent wrote in his diary about the black tracker "Worthless native who had been given power over his own native people and had absconded in the night. Presumed gone, a term the Natives use is 'walkabout'." The other older Nyoongars knew what had actually happened, but their lips were sealed, even to their own people.

Edward Jackie Singer was a tribal leader. His hate for the black trackers was very notable in his manner of speech and actions. But his hate didn't only focus on the native trackers, but also on the white people, who disrupted the Nyoongars' life style. They say he also killed two white people on a lonely track in the dense scrub around the Moora area. Their bodies and pack horses were never found. The authorities had searched for months in the thick terrain looking for their bodies and pack horses but to no avail. The authorities presumed that they had simply vanished, even got lost on their journey to the Goldfields on their search for gold.

Edward Jackie Singer was finally captured and shot by the people he hated the most, the white troopers and their counterparts, the black trackers. Seeing that he was branded a renegade by the officials, his body was left to rot in the bush where it belonged. No funeral, nothing, but to be left to the dingoes, crows and lizards to feast on.

Nora brushed tears from her eyes and looked directly at the faces of her children. The two faces had a look of overwhelming disbelief.

"Did they find his bones?" gasped Ted, looking frantically at his sister, who had been weeping softly.

"Yeah, dey did find his bones. He be ol' fella, he be name Warrnball. He be the last of the ol' warriors, too smart for white policeman an black trackers. Dey bin neber catch him."

"Did he bury Grandad's bones?" asked Jill sniffling.

"Yeah, he buried your Grandad's bones around Moora, New Norcia Mission or Moore River

Settlement or around Mogumber somewhere. That area, you know? Ol' man Warrnball took my father's burial secret to his grave. No one knows where he is buried, only ol' Warrnball, an he dead, too, long time."

"Oh, Mum," cried Jill, rushing across to hold her Mum. "How can people be so cruel! Why didn't these white people sit down and talk about this country with our ancestors, instead of just seizing, demanding, maiming and killing for what was not rightfully theirs, anyhow. Have they no heart!"

Ted got up and went over to his mother and sister. Putting an arm around their shoulders, he spoke with authority. "The time will come when past injustices will be acknowledged and I can almost see it now, as my father and grandfather walk together in peace in God's own garden."

The wailing of the two females within the walls of the room even brought a tear to Ted's eye, as they all held each other and let the tears flow.

Glossary of Nyoongar Words

barrl – him/her/he
boojarri – pregnant
boyyah – money
bulyaka – take off, go
buntji/buntji man – womaniser
cartwarra – mad/silly
choo – shame
gerbah – alcohol
gnoonie/gnoonies – brother/brothers
gnumeerie/gnumeeries – cigarettes or tobacco
gobberl – stomach
koordah/koord – brother
moorditj – very good
jerripin – happy good/solid
mubbarn man – doctor man or shaman
munartj – police
muntj – sexual intercourse
ni ni – listen

noorn – sad

Nyoongar/s – South-west Aborigine/s of Western Australia

tjulep – loin cloth used to cover private parts

tuppy – female private parts/vagina

unna – wanting agreement/could be question

warra – bad/evil

watjella – white person

Wongki/Wongi – Goldfields Aborigine/s

Yamitji/Yamitjis – North-west Aborigine/s

yanbi – incorrect/improper

yonga – kangaroo

yorgah – woman/girl

yortj – penis

Adnyamathanha people from around the Flinders Ranges in South Australia and they spoke the Yura Ngawarla.

Acknowledgements

To Reverend Selin Garlett and his wife, Marilyn, who encouraged and supported me to complete the last few remaining stories and were there in my hour of need.

To Dr Anne Brewster, who suggested I put some of my work in the anthology, *Those who remain will always remember* which encouraged me to complete these short stories.

To Ruth and Wayne Phelan, with whom I stayed in Cunderdin and who also encouraged and supported me with "Uncle Jacko" and "The Wool Pickers." I made a lot of friends there, especially Ruth and Wayne. We had a lot of good laughs with Reddog and Cleo

To my son, Alfred Arron, who listened intently after school and gave me encouragement with lovely words on hearing my first story "Granny Daisy". His words of "dus solid, Dad" or "dus a moorditj story, Dad," inspired me with the other short stories.

To my daughter, Janice Marie, on seeing her

arrival into the world on a warm tropical night in Townsville, North Queensland, inspired me to write "The Best Night of My Life."

To Tazuko Kaino and Kandese Garstone, who were always there at Magabala Books to type out my hand-written stories – a big thank you.

To Peter Bibby, who was there from the start at Magabala Books, from my first story to my last. Thank you for all the encouragement and support over the years.

To Maureen Comley, who had no hesitation in typing out my last few remaining copies and although there were a few Nyoongar words in the stories, it did not dampen her enthusiasm or integrity.

To the staff of Magabala Books both past and present. You stuck with me for a "Long Time Now." Thank you.

To all those wonderful people who inspired me to put all these stories together around a flagon and some gunja, around some park, be it in Perth, Adelaide, Brisbane or Kalgoorlie. A park is a blackfella's delight.

Alf Taylor
2001